My People's Waltz

My People's Waltz

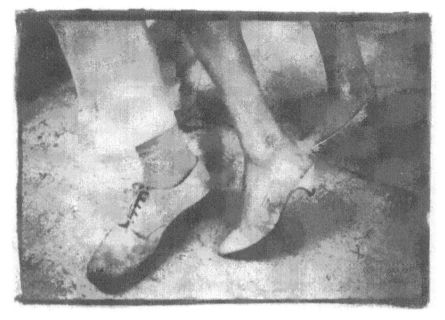

Dale Ray Phillips

W. W. NORTON & COMPANY / NEW YORK / LONDON

"Why I'm Talking" and "What Men Love For" appeared in the *Atlantic*.
"The Woods at the Back of Our Houses" appeared in *Harper's*.
"At the Edge of the New World" appeared in *Ploughshares*.
"Everything Quiet Like Church," "Corporal Love," and "What We Are Up Against"
    appeared in *Story*.
"What Men Love For" also appeared in *The Best American Short Stories of 1989*.
"Everything Quiet Like Church" also appeared in *New Stories from the South: The Year's Best
    1995*.
"Corporal Love" also appeared in *New Stories from the South: The Year's Best 1997*.
"When Love Gets Worn" appeared in *GQ*.
"What It Cost Travelers" appeared in *The Greensboro Review*.

For information about permission to reproduce selections from this book,
write to Permissions, W. W. Norton & Company, Inc.,
500 Fifth Avenue, New York, NY 10110.

The text of this book is composed in Bembo
with the display set in Tiffany
Composition and manufacturing by The Haddon Craftsmen, Inc.
Book design by JAM Design
Title page photograph by Carol Ford.

Library of Congress Cataloging-in-Publication Data
    My people's waltz / by Dale Ray Phillips.
        p.   cm.
    ISBN 978-0-393-34290-1
    1. Southern States—Social life and customs—Fiction.   I. Title.
PS3566.H4765M9   1999
813'.54—dc21   98-37090
                                                         CIP

W. W. Norton & Company, Inc., 500 Fifth Avenue, New York, N.Y. 10110
                http://www.wwnorton.com

W. W. Norton & Company Ltd., 10 Coptic Street, London WC1A 1PU

1 2 3 4 5 6 7 8 9 0

Acknowledgments

I WOULD like to thank three maestros—Doris Betts, Fred Chappell, and Jim Whitehead. I am also indebted to my friends at The Skybox and Roger's Recreation Hall. Thanks should be extended to Jill Bialosky, who made this book possible. Special appreciation is also intended for George Singleton, Dixon Boyles, Susan Tekulve, Harold Woodell, Jeannie McGee, Michael Gills, Ron Rash, Bart Barton, and the inestimable Jim Clark—all fine writers and steadfast friends.

Sloan Harris deserves a paragraph to himself for his patience with me and his doggedness that this book see print.

Stephen Ford and Amanda McKeel and my love for them should also be given due respect and good notice.

Contents

For my daughter, Ivy Elizabeth Phillips,
and for all the loved ones
these three names evoke.

My People's Waltz

But I hung on like death:
Such waltzing was not easy.
                —Theodore Roethke, *My Papa's Waltz*

Why I'm Talking

for Otto Salassi

MY GRANDFATHER kept his floozy in a silver Airstream above the bend in the river where the dead crossed over. He had finagled Miss Minnie a job as lifetime caretaker of a little patch of no-man's-land and a cemetery just across the Haw River. Whenever a black tenant farmer died, we watched from the trailer's picture window as a slipshod barge fashioned of dye-barrel pontoons and salvaged lumber ferried the coffin and mourners across the river to the grave. On these occasions Miss Minnie usually fried catfish from the deep freezer, which we kept chock-full by trotlining. The passage of a neighbor to the other shore dispirited her, but it made my grandfather hungry.

"There goes another soul to sweet Jesus," Miss Minnie would remark.

"Not to Jesus," my grandfather would say, correcting her. "To a place not listed on any of the maps."

The cemetery was part of a deal concocted by my grandfather. The property had been willed as a Negro cemetery by an eccentric widow whose ancestor had kept slaves and whose land straddled two counties—neither of which wanted the expense of an additional black graveyard. My grandfather, a retired circuit judge and back-room dealmaker, persuaded both counties to lease the dead woman's land to black tenant tobacco farmers and apply the rents to graveyard maintenance. Because neither county acknowledged the site's existence, and because the site was so rural, no bridge had been funded. This was North Carolina in the sixties; my family was white; and my grandfather's solution to the rural Negro burial problem both relieved his party's white constituency and bestowed on him near-hero status among country blacks. It also gave him a place not listed on any of the municipal maps to safekeep Miss Minnie, who was the only black woman with red hair and freckles I had ever seen.

I was eight that summer, and had decided to stop talking. My reasoning seemed sound enough: whatever had abducted my mother might steal me if I let out too many words. *Don't tell,* she had said the afternoon I last saw her. She wore her bridal gown and talked nonstop to her reflection in the mirror. After dusk she instructed me to sit on her lap as she made hand shadows, the shapes in turn as fierce and friendly and unnameable as her craziness. Her heart drummed against my spine, and I understood that we were at a juncture for which neither of us could find words. My father returned from work and got to us before the oven's gas did. "I hope it's not hereditary," he said as he drove me to my grandfather's "real" house in Graham—a columned stone residence listed in the historical register, where my mother had been born and where her mother, when alive, had entertained governors. I would stay with my grandfather while my father worked as a traveling x-ray-machine salesman and my mother recuperated at an oceanside hospital. "What's the matter—why aren't you talking?" first my father and then my grandfather asked. I didn't answer, because I was still in that wordless place in our lives. My father and grandfather went into the study to discuss strategies. I do not know what went on in that room, but I soon learned I would live with my grandfather where the dead crossed over while my mother was away.

"Not talking don't make you special," said Sudie, Miss Minnie's illegitimate fifteen-year-old daughter. "Give me an Indian head and get your feel." We slept in the same bed that summer, and for a nickel she'd let me knead and suckle her breasts. We never had anything close to sex; what we did was more like playing doctor, but with a consultation fee. Sudie provided my earliest education in metaphysics: she believed, among other things, that a chicken's claw touched to a sleeper's forehead gave you power over that person; that spiders wove into their webs the names of people who would die violently; and that on certain nights—especially the summer solstice and Halloween—you could look into the Haw, and under the mirrored surface the faces of everyone who had ever lived would drift by, caught in the silent place from which the dead watch us.

Sometimes at night, while my grandfather and Miss Minnie slept, Sudie and I sneaked from the trailer and lay on the barge, waiting for Willie Reese. Sudie told stories while an owl hooted from an empty place out in the night. The river was always the setting of these stories, involving the back seats of battered sedans and subsequent shotgun weddings, snakebites, moonshine, unfaithful lovers and stabbings, ghosts, and lunatic relatives who tried to drown themselves. Sudie allowed me to light a crooked Salem she kept hidden in her underwear. The dirt path leading up to the bluff and trailer shone like snow in the full moon's light, and from this direction Willie Reese would strut, seeming a piece of the night scissored free and set to walking.

"My Sudie baby out here waiting for Willie Reese?" His voice was as slick and twisted as licorice as he stepped on board the

barge. When he saw me, his face formed a question and then re-
laxed. He considered me a conspirator, as most people did; when
you don't talk, people assume you won't tell.

"Up by the fork in the road there's a sack of candy for a fellow who knows how to keep his mouth shut." Willie Reese got
nervous if I watched him and Sudie make love. I trotted to where
the driveway branched off the dirt road, and I found the candy.
Then I peed my initials in the dirt. Our front yard was a half acre
of tobacco, and I wandered between the rows. From my pocket
I took the map my father had given me, with a red circle marking his territory in the mountains, and a blue circle indicating my
mother's hospital, at the ocean. I'd try to think of anything but
my suspicion that love had gotten us into all this. I stretched myself atop the map to encompass the places my parents were scattered. Then I thought of small miracles: the way peppermint
tasted of winter and things lingering; the sound my name—
Richard—made as it came back at me after I had shouted it
down a well; the gritty taste of red clay Miss Minnie had secretly
made me eat to cure my muteness; the coaxing of a chicken to
sleep by forcing its head to the sand and drawing a line with a
stick outward from its beak; and the gradual way the water rose
after upstream, unseen thundershowers. When this happened,
the river sounded the way the wind does when it weaves a net
of itself through the trees. At such times the Haw seemed the
oldest of hymns, forcing the measure of its music into us all.

THIS WAS the summer I learned that guile was not necessarily
bad or verbal. Once a week my grandfather and I dressed in our
best suits and returned to Graham—where his house sat across
from the courthouse. We feigned the look of travelers returning
hurriedly to conduct domestic business. My grandfather opened
and answered his mail and assured meddlesome neighbors that
the specialists in Chapel Hill—where we were supposedly stay-

ing—were making headway against my speechlessness. The most doting and double-chinned of the widows, Cleora Cates, actually cried when my grandfather explained that my treatment consisted of a series of painful abdominal shots like the ones victims of rabies endure. Family histories were recounted: somehow our predicament—my grandmother's death two years earlier and my mother's nervousness—reminded these women of similar tribulations that life had visited upon them. A sort of collective speculation on why God permits evil seemed to connect us all. The booty that came from nodding a sad yes to all that my grandfather manufactured was armfuls of black-walnut cakes and chess pies and fresh cobblers. The lesson I learned was twofold and simple: once something is uttered, it takes on a life of its own; and sadness must be fed. On each of these visits I wrote my mother postcards, dictated by my grandfather, about the kindly specialists in Chapel Hill and the good life on Courthouse Square. We posted these dispatches weekly in lieu of phone calls, because my silence hindered her recovery. Deception and protection would be forever linked for me.

"Jesus," my grandfather said as we drove back to our hideaway. I was eating blackberry cobbler straight from the casserole dish with three cupped fingers. "Can you see me marrying one of those old bats? It would be all slippers and Rook games and goddamned church socials. And you—they'd have you taking piano lessons and singing in the Rotary Boys' Club Choir."

Another time he said, "Richard, when you sort things out and start talking again, what will you say? That you had a dandy time this summer?" I had. "That unconscionable acts were committed in the trailer?" I had once walked in on him and Miss Minnie, catching them in what I would later learn to call *flagrante delicto*. "Whatever else you say"—he hammered on the wheel as the judge in him talked—"explain that social circumstances prevented an outright and public declaration of my feelings toward

Miss Minnie." Like most people in love, my grandfather thought his predicament was beyond explanation.

WHENEVER THE signs in *Grier's Almanac* were propitious, Miss Minnie administered spells and potions to cure me of my voluntary muteness. I endured necklaces of garlic, an impromptu exorcism in which I stared at a crucifix so long I feared my eyes had permanently crossed, several smelly poultices strapped snugly to my chest like life jackets, and baptisms in everything from mailorder holy water to motor oil. Miss Minnie had once cured a dog of mange by rubbing it with Quaker State, so she tried it on me. Healing me became secondary only to her duties as mistress. My grandfather usually watched us from the hammock with his two-o'clock toddy resting on his generous belly. He alone seemed to sense that my silence was a protective measure against the force that scattered the things I loved.

"The boy is simply making an existential statement," he'd say after his third or fourth bourbon. "His silence is his defense." Then he got that look in his eye of a man on vacation who suddenly remembers the small pleasures of afternoon baths and naps. He announced that the heat and whiskey had given him mild heart palpitations; would Miss Minnie do him the honor of giving him an alcohol chest rub in the bedroom by the window fan? Sudie and I checked the trotlines while they made love. From the johnboat's bow the trailer resembled the balcony my mother had waved from when my father and I had taken her to the hospital, and above that—past the canopy of oaks so old the area's first settlers and Indians had negotiated treaties beneath those limbs at this natural ford in the river—stretched the blue promise of heaven. *Above us all, there is healing,* I'd think.

This belief and the river formed the architecture of my childhood. The Haw in June was as sluggish as a cat in a favorite chair. While Sudie poled, I handlined for small bream beneath weeping willows. We baited our trotline with these fish. Down past the bend in the river where the barge crossed, we set our line, weighted at intervals with bricks. As I walked the line, the catfish came up slowly—white-bellied ghosts whose sudden materialization I felt in throbs before I saw them. In trotlining, as in all fishing, the participant evokes an unspoken order. If each hook is baited properly and set at the right depth, a predictable event—a caught fish—will follow, and a wholeness seemed secured whenever we ate what we caught. Things were too often unpredictable; I understood this at eight, but I couldn't articulate it. My mother's absence was a mystery, as was the reason that Sudie's breasts soothed me; yet somehow I had traveled to this place not known to cartographers, on a river whose flowing defined its being. While I unhooked the catfish and dispatched them with a jackknife blade to the brain, Sudie explained the way water worked its way down from the sky and through earth and bedrock and the graves of the dead to become a substance solid enough to float the boat where we fished. And she told stories. Many of her tales were repetitive and inconsistent; in one version her first lover might be Willie Reese, while in another it was the retarded Stutgart boy. How can something be two things? I'd wonder.

At the crossroads store—where we went almost every evening with my grandfather after trotlining—my dumbness became a source of betting and speculation. Porter Satterfield laid ten dollars on a hunch that nights, in my sleep, I chattered away with all my held-in words wanting out. Lincoln Coble theorized that my condition was the result of a curse that a man condemned to hang had levied against my grandfather, the sentencing judge. My grandfather reminded him that no one had been hanged in our two counties for more than two hundred years, and that until recently the boys in Raleigh had done the executing by electric chair. This fact—death by electricity—set off stories of downed power lines and ball lightning, which had once rolled through Stan Snow's shotgun hallway. Specific dates of catastrophic storms would be argued not in calendar terms such as July 24, 1955, but in terms of events, such as three weeks after the Waller boy died of swine flu. Sitting there and listening, I was amazed that my misfortune was a part of their own. We were a hard people, who counted time by tragedies and who took a storyteller's pleasure in reshaping our sadness.

THE ONLY time my father visited, he brought a nurse named Darlene. She French-inhaled her cigarette and tugged down the hem of her uniform, which snapped as he guided her from his Buick to the cinder-block steps where I sat halfway through the crew cut Miss Minnie was inflicting. When he opened his arms to me, I pressed my face to his chest, finding his sweat-and-starched-shirt smell mixed with perfume. My father's hand admired the bristled portion of my head and gauged the inches I had grown. When he pinched the muscle I made, he whistled admiringly. Had he brought this woman to cure me?

"Cat still got your tongue?" he asked.

"Look at what the dogs dragged in." My grandfather, dripping wet and in his boxers, struggled with the last tricky steps of the railroad-tie path that led up from the river, where he took his daily bath on sunny days though we had a tub. He tipped back Miss Minnie's sunbonnet, which protected his bald head, and squinted with weak eyes at our strange little group. His long walking stick, fashioned of a sapling once twisted by kudzu, made him resemble a shepherd.

"Confound it, Minnie, don't just stand there—get me my glasses," he said to Darlene. Minnie left us standing in the awkwardness of the moment and returned with his spectacles and his favorite bathrobe, embroidered with peacocks. The tenuous mo-

ment was lengthened as he put on his glasses and evaluated what
he saw. Once, my mother had stood before a mirror and taken
our picture, and the way my grandfather surveyed us reminded
me of the way my own eyes had doubted what they saw.

"Whoa, now. What's this?" my grandfather asked.

"Darlene here works third shift at a hospital in Asheville," my
father explained. "She needed a lift to the beach, and as I was
headed that way, because the doctors said a four-day outing and
a second honeymoon with my wife was in order, I offered Darlene my services."

"Your services," my grandfather said. "I bet you offered her
your services."

"You're a fine one to judge." My father pointed at Sudie, walking up from the river wearing a necklace of catfish. The tension
vanished when my grandfather remarked what an odd lot we all
were: a girl wearing fish, a boy half-haired and half-shorn, a man
with a nurse in tow, and himself in wet boxers and a bathrobe—
all as dumb as stones to be standing like this in the hot sun. Sudie
hung the fish on the skinning spike and came over to hug my
grandfather. He laughed at her with the same laugh he had for
me whenever I amused him, and I understood that I had known
she was his daughter for a while now—just as my parents' late-
night arguments had announced that women like Darlene existed
in the world where my father traveled. *It's like a charm bracelet,*
Sudie had said the first time she showed me how to string and
wear the fish so that the dorsal fins would not prick and infect
me with venom. *It keeps the river from pulling you into its world.* The
fishy odor of daily trotlining never quite left our skins, and in bed
at night I breathed its comforting secrets with my nose flattened
against the brown warmness of Sudie's breasts the way I had
once pressed my face to a winter windowpane to witness my
breath made visible as it dissipated. This was my first concept of

the force that took things away. Sudie claimed that a breath was the same stuff as clouds—water caught between heaven and earth.

"I'm as dry as a desert," my father said. We moved to the picnic table, stationed in the ragged shade of an ancient sycamore whose roots had buckled our attempts at a brick patio. The still air hummed with cicadas as we shooed botflies from our faces. Miss Minnie finished shearing me while Sudie was sent inside to punch out crustless chicken-salad sandwiches with a jelly jar. The company jar of white liquor made by the Kenny boys was stood on the table. Miss Minnie and Darlene laced theirs with lemonade, while my father and grandfather bumped theirs back medicinally. When Sudie whined that she never got to taste the stuff, I received a dollop in my Nehi soda too. If I was my mother's son, the joke went, *that* would get me to jabbering. I sat on my father's knee as the two men talked of points of mutual interest: when my mother's recovery could be expected (by the end of August, the doctors had assured my father); whether I would travel to the beach this weekend to visit her (no—my mother was adamant that I not see her in a hospital); whether Darlene's presence meant that my father was pulling out on his family ("Don't be absurd," he said). Then the two men began planning a family vacation on Hatteras Island as soon as my mother recuperated. It was as if two worlds existed—an old one where your origins lay, which you hid, and a new one over which you speculated hopefully.

Miss Minnie and Darlene helped themselves to more liquor and ignored the other lives my father and grandfather were discussing. They talked of hard times: before my grandfather, Miss Minnie had been kept by a doctor who beat her and insisted that she dress like an Indian princess. Darlene matched Minnie's story with the insight that certain men liked nurse's uniforms. Then she confided that she was running from an ex-husband whose temper had landed her in the hospital more than once. The mention of hospitals made me think of my mother and of a happy time while vacationing at the ocean, before her full-blown nervousness. My father had heaved out the big rod for drum, but the surf had washed the heavy line shoreward. I had just learned to swim, and when a length of line drifted by, I dove under and tugged like a great fish. This was my first adult-sized deception. I surfaced as far from the line as my breath would allow, and saw my father jerking the rod as he tried to set the hook. My mother laughed and pointed at my father with her drink as she signaled with a finger over her lips that she was in on the shenanigans. The surf had worn off the unattended bait, but my father showed us the bare hook as proof that a monstrous drum had stolen his cut mullet. That night my father insisted that we feast on steaks *and* shrimp at a restaurant where he told the waitress he had wrestled with a man-eating shark. Then a couple three tables over speculated that the fish was an amberjack—they had seen them schooling in the surf that very morning. Grave discussions followed on the nature of the beast my father had grappled with. Even the busboy offered his opinion. When we left, patrons waved and wished us luck. That night there had seemed no more secure a confederacy than the spoken and silent portions of our love. This woman, Darlene, threatened to lure my father away.

I waited until my father and grandfather had gone to check the Buick's oil and Miss Minnie was inside seasoning the pintos with Sudie before I slipped Darlene the picture of my mother I had been harboring. Then I ran to the river and shed my clothes for a swim. I practiced all the strokes I knew—jellyfish, sidestroke, crawl, under water, and backstroke. The joke in the family was that I was half fish. When I found a rock big enough and jumped off the barge with it, the weight carried me past where the light quit, to a place I feared was bottomless. All the way down, the words and air escaped in bubbles until my feet found the riverbed. With the stone on my chest, I lay back and imitated someone dead. While my ears popped, I felt with a free hand for a souvenir pebble from this place where everything uttered sounded like Beelzebub. I talked to my mother, saying "I have gone to the bottom of the world and brought this back for you." This childish fantasy continued as long as my lungs lasted. I invented yarns of successfully skirted tragedies and open-armed homecomings. The force that had taken my mother, I was convinced, could be cajoled into giving her back.

Though I had expected to find my father, angry that I had shown his traveling companion the picture, Darlene stood on the barge when I surfaced. She seemed relieved that I hadn't drowned.

"Your mother?" She tucked the picture into the pocket of my pants, which were lying neatly folded on the decking. She claimed that the liquor and sun made her feel like dancing, so she pulled off her shoes without untying them and held an imaginary partner at arm's length as she waltzed. The loneliness of talking under water and of slow dancing alone struck me. For some reason I wanted this woman to see me naked. I pulled myself onto the barge, and she wrapped me in the towel I kept on the railing. I dressed with my front to her and stood for her approval.

"I didn't want to meet you," she said. "Men get a strange pleasure from such things. Once, I dated a man who made me eat every Friday night in the same restaurant where he and his wife were having supper. I swear, it's like they say—love me for the lies I tell. But you . . ." she smiled. "You're a little man who doesn't talk. Thanks for showing me your mother's picture."

I imagined Darlene and my father speeding toward the ocean with the wind from the open windows parting their hair in odd places. Would they honk at passing cars, or stop for beer and barbecue, as we did when en route to the ocean?

"Don't worry," Darlene added as an afterthought. "I don't steal men. I just let them be boys for a while until they're ready to be men again." When she stirred her drink with her finger, the way my mother did, I began blubbering.

"There, now," Darlene said. "There, now." She pulled me close enough to smell my father's Old Spice on her uniform, and I buried my head where my father's had been. Here was a disconsolate smell I hoped never to inherit.

THREE DAYS later my mother escaped from her second honeymoon with my father, and on the summer solstice she unearthed our whereabouts. Their reconciliation had ended when my father walked from the rented cottage to the pier for cigarettes and returned to find my mother and the car gone. I was alone in the trailer when he called at midnight. My grandfather and Miss Minnie had gone on a moonlight stroll to ease the numbness in his left side, which he attributed to bursitis and inactivity. Sudie had sneaked to the tobacco barn, where she had been spending much time lately, making me nod yes, I would stay in bed. She promised we would hunt ghosts later that night, when everyone was asleep.

"Who am I talking to? Do I have the right number?" my father kept asking. Then he understood. "Bump once on the receiver if it's you." I did. "Is everyone gone?" I bumped once for yes. "Damn." Then he explained that he was hurrying toward Graham, where my mother's good-bye note indicated she was headed. He had rented a car and would intercept her there. He said my grandfather and I should get back to Courthouse Square and normal living that very night. "Get there before she does, and make the house look lived in." She had an hour's jump on him, so he would have to rush. Things needed to seem normal when she got there—did I understand that? I did. More than anything, I was to quit this no-talking nonsense and explain to my grandfather the urgency of the situation. Then my father tried to coerce me into speaking. When he asked if I wanted my mother to be upset, I tapped twice to show that I didn't. "She will if she finds out about all this. Say something," he said. I answered by disconnecting the phone cord from the wall. This was in the time of party lines, and I imagined my father's panic when he called again and an angry neighbor finally answered our ring and reminded him how late it was.

LATER, IN bed, after everyone else had fallen asleep, Sudie explained that this was the night the dead ranged like cats searching for lost lives. With money in a jar you could catch a spirit, because spirits put coins on their eyes to pay for safe passage between worlds. This seemed as logical to me as the Resurrection, or the common belief that on each anniversary of the instant of Christ's birth, barnyard animals briefly possessed the power of speech. We would catch ourselves a ghost and bribe it into answering questions. She claimed that this enterprise was expensive: my life's savings—a Mason jar heavy with silver hoarded from birthdays, allowances, and odd jobs—might be required. I had been saving the money to buy a brother who would talk for me. That money was *meant* to be stolen.

"You get a free feel tonight," Sudie said. I had placed the customary nickel in her palm. She had been secretive lately, hiding tins of Spam and inventorying her wardrobe. For the past two weeks she had refused to allow me to visit the barge with her, and when she returned, with first light, she muffled her crying with a pillow.

To catch and question a ghost, you need a store of money, a bend in the river that ghosts travel, a guide familiar with their habits, and a belief that the language they have mastered is kin to your own. *When you die,* I had told my mother that day I sat in her lap by the open oven, *I want you to remember me.* I did not understand that I was breathing the same gas. Now, it is I who remember my people and that summer they staked claim to me.

Down on the barge I dangled my legs in the water while Sudie took the johnboat and the jar of silver across the Haw. Distant heat lightning illuminated the shoreline without a sound. The glow from the lantern bobbled up and down as she poled. A mist so thick I could swirl handfuls of it rose from the river, full of mint and the promising odor of bream. When Sudie's lantern disappeared behind the headstones in the cemetery, I lay back on the deck and practiced masturbating—something I had seen the Banther boys do over girlie pictures in their cardboard-and-canvas clubhouse. I took comfort in the newfound feel of my stiffness and in the patterns cast on the treetops by headlights on the highway past the tobacco field. *Hell's bells, hell's bells, hell's bells,* I thought, for that was what the Banther boys had said. I knew my earnest manipulation would lead me to an urgency, but it was still beyond me at eight. Tired of this exploration, I zippered myself and searched the river for some sign of ghostly passages.

"I know where a bag of peppermints can be found by a fellow who can keep his mouth shut." When Willie Reese stepped onto the barge, he laughed at how thoroughly he had scared me. He sported a traveling suit with a feathered hat and a wicker suitcase bound with a strap. He glanced over his shoulder nervously, as if being followed. I shook my head no when he asked if I had seen any ghosts. He claimed that as a professional spirit chaser, he could get positive results. He would ferry the barge over to Sudie, bait a jar with snake oil, stopper it when a ghost went inside for a taste, and bring back the jar for me to keep. I would be the only person in Alamance County with a soul in a jar. Like a regular Aladdin's lamp, he claimed, this soul would grant me three wishes.

"You realize you'll have to start talking to make those wishes." Willie Reese had unhitched the barge and taken off for Sudie and what I now realize was the rest of their life together. They would float downriver to the first town with a bus station and vanish from our lives. They eloped with my hoarded innocence into whatever happiness they would own, and I have been following them ever since.

My grandfather was awake and drinking when I tried to sneak back inside. He held up each glassful to the globed ceiling light for inspection before swallowing. "Sudie and that Reese boy are lucky," he said, and I understood that he had allowed her to elope. "We're caught, thanks to your phone trick." The phone had been reattached and moved beside the chair that Miss Minnie kept stationed for my grandfather to place and accept calls. I had forgotten that Minnie always checked for a dial tone before going to bed, in case an emergency occurred. My grandfather explained that my father had caught up with my mother in Graham. "When she suspected where we were, it took all he could do to persuade her not to notify the police and charge me with kidnapping. When I talked to her, she was threatening to have *me* institutionalized for bringing you here. I couldn't see the sense in pretending anymore that this place doesn't exist, so she's on her way out." My clothes were packed in boxes stacked head high by the door. His suitcases were beside them, with shirttails sticking out. Broken figurines covered the coffee table, and I realized that the car was gone, along with Miss Minnie. Whoever had done this had left in an angry exodus.

"Minnie finally understood that she shouldn't be here when your mother and father arrive," he said when I picked up a glass unicorn. "I've got friends in Danville who'll look after her until this blows over." He rubbed his sternum. "I've also got one hell of a case of heartburn and one hell of an angry and crazy daughter headed my way. I just thought some wild time on the river would get you out of this speak-no-evil mood. You see, your mother knew all about Miss Minnie and this place—even *her* mother did. They just never confronted me with its existence. It's you who didn't know about it. My heart—" he said, and I expected the story of the time it had done leapfrogs inside his chest when he had first seen Minnie. Instead he clawed at his T-shirt and toppled backward so hard that when the straight-backed chair hit the linoleum, his head bounced twice. The swiftness of a heart attack amazed me. His feet pedaled in the air for a bicycle that wasn't there. As the last convulsions struck, he bit off a portion of his tongue. His eyes became as wide as things held under a magnifying glass, and I searched for my image in them as they clouded. Then I shut my grandfather's eyes, because I didn't want to see what they saw.

What do you do with your forefather's tongue? I put that tip of tongue to my lips, stood in front of the living-room mirror, and made it waggle. When pulled away, it left a little moustache of blood. Here was a thing that had lived and loved and pronounced judgments—and it was mine. Then I weighted it with rocks fetched from my river-bottoming and bound the whole affair with cheesecloth meant to wrap fish heads and seasonings for catfish stew. I hurried to the Haw and heaved in this strange offering, because I feared becoming fluent in the language it now spoke.

MY FATHER and mother caught me in the bathroom, naked, trying to wash what I knew from my body. She started screaming when she walked into the trailer and saw her father's corpse, and ran from room to room as she called my name. "Thank God," she said when she found me in the tub. She moaned my grandfather's name and sat on the toilet with her head between her legs while my father fed her pills and whiskey at intervals. Soon she retreated to that sleepy, protected place where he kept her so he wouldn't lose her. He said he had checked the pulse, and now he must call the coroner. He left the bathroom with strict instructions to stay put and be safe. My mother stroked my hair without remarking that she had never seen me with a crew cut. She said therapy made remembering things difficult. "Another person was in me," she claimed, "but she left." She dreamily explained that she had always wanted to visit this place but she never had, and she was tired of it now—it was much shabbier than she had expected. As she talked, she seemed the ghost of my childhood unfettering itself.

The truth of that summer would get absorbed into the story that we would live. When we left the trailer, we would pretend that summer didn't exist. *If you tell,* my father had warned before I disconnected him, *you are a part of all this.* He came in now with more bourbon and shut the door with his back against it like a sentry. After another glass my mother began insisting that the doctors had cured her, and that the best thing to do was to put all this behind us and use the inheritance money to build in a new subdivision being planned along the upper reaches of the Haw. My father seconded the opinion and voiced certain complaints against a man as supposedly honorable as a judge who carted a *child* along on jaunts to a bimbo. He looked hard at me and swore he had no idea we were holed up here. I understood that we would blame all this on my grandfather.

My parents talked excitedly of the future—the business of the living. I listened—the business of children who one day wish to tell. As my father talked of new beginnings, his voice carried the conviction that my mother should be kept safe from the world of Darlenes, where men died in trailers. He was full of the contagious hopefulness people adopt when disaster forces them to start over. The ways we all learned to hurt one another in later years were distant odds we were betting we could beat. I sat, unashamed of my nakedness, in that tub, listening to the new world my parents promised as I bothered the tan marks on my ankles which a summer's worth of sun had left above my shod feet. Then I pulled the plug and lowered my finger into the empty space created by water funneling out the drain. If Sudie was right, this water would enter and exit granite and get caught up as air and the green urge of spring buds. It would christen babies and make hoses hiss and fill space enough for couples on ocean liners to travel. Some of this water was already conspiring to become the dark color of the bend in the river where the dead crossed over. Just as water renamed itself as it entered all things, we would redefine ourselves like a twice-told tale. In that trailer by the river we were that close to where one thing becomes another—which is what the dead see.

"What happened, what happened?" my mother asked. I understood that although this periodic leave-taking had already become a part of our lives, we had somehow become a family, caught in the awkwardness of shaping our first reunion as we reinvented the story of the rest of our lives together. Some chimeras would have to be constructed to keep this good feeling alive, and so I answered her with this voice, which love had taught to deceive.

What Men Love For

WHEN I was twelve, my father called on weeknights to convince my mother that he would return safely that weekend and to assure himself that his house was still in order. The phone's ringing always startled my mother from what she was doing—blowing smoke rings through the window screen, or, when she was extremely melancholy, cutting her face out of old pictures of herself. The calls sent her swiftly to the bathroom, where she locked the door and gargled. She had returned home that spring after another nervous breakdown, and she believed that each ring meant my father had driven off some mountainside or had abandoned us because she was a manic-depressive. Her worst fear was that he was calling from a pay phone somewhere past the Appalachians, to say he was on his way to sunny and golden California.

"Richard," my father said one night. "You keeping the home motor tuned and purring for your old man?" Our weekend hobby was restoring motorcycles. "How's the chrome tank on that Harley coming along? You got the rust spots off yet?"

"Everything's as shiny as a new dime," I said.

"And your mother. You would tell me if something was wrong again?"

"Old Buck's got everything under control," I said. Buck Rogers was my father's childhood hero, and he trusted me when I called myself that.

"You can count on old Buck." My mother picked up the bedroom extension. My father explained to her that when he came home that weekend, we would grill steaks and make ice cream.

"By God, we might even break out the old Satchmo records and some wine, and dance in the kitchen. Have us a cozy little party with the lights turned low."

My father addressed me, on the kitchen extension. "Hey, Richard. They called your old man Fleet Foot back in the days when dancing was dancing." There on the kitchen table my mother had carefully aligned the cut-out faces in one row and the pictures in another. And then my father was rambling again, saying that he was up for a promotion, which would mean less traveling. "After Labor Day, I should be home two days a week, plus weekends. Two or three years of that and who knows?" His dream was to quit traveling through North Carolina, where we lived, and Virginia. He presented my mother with a version of how life would be once he got the right breaks and became the owner of his own hospital-supply company. "I'd be home every night. The business would be shaky at first, but hell, all businesses are. Ours would be a family enterprise that *worked*. We'd all take an interest in it, make decisions together, things like that."

"You can count old Buck in," I said.

"What about now?" my mother asked.

"Labor Day," my father said. "Let me snag that promotion and I'll be home more. Is that too much to ask?"

"I suppose not." My mother hung up her extension. I said the good-byes for us both. I put the faces and the pictures they'd come from into the photograph box, and then I retrieved a sleeping pill from the supply I kept hidden. I went to where my mother lay in bed, gave her one, and turned the fan on low.

"You have to stop doing this," I said.

"It helps when I feel bad." I had a difficult time understanding what had happened to the woman who had once laughed and clapped as I walked around the kitchen on my hands, saying to her, "This is how they walk in China—upside down," the change tumbling from my pockets. She had been glum and anxious since coming back. "Please don't tell," she had said when I first caught her cutting her face from the pictures. She held the photograph to her face, looking at me through an image of herself, eye blinking and peering where her face had been. At the time I was afraid that my father would guess that her nervousness had returned, and that they would take her away again. These secrets from my father held us together.

"Can we do cat's cradle?" she asked. She had folded her robe over a chair beside the bed, and she took the string from its pocket. I sat beside her and played cat's cradle. The twine slipped from her hands to mine and then back, each exchange making a different configuration. As she slipped into sleep, I made Jacob's ladder, weaving a narrow net of string twisted taut between my fingers. We were strings of a fragile ladder, working in collusion with and against each other.

THE COOL portion of each morning, I set up a ladder before the dew had evaporated, when no one was stirring on our street except the milkman and husbands taking out the garbage before leaving for work. My job was to reglaze a third-floor window. I learned the simple but universal law that craftsmen somehow know—that working with your hands is a pleasure, especially work so mindless that everything you need to forget becomes absorbed by the sash to be mended. This law's implication is that in routing out a bad strip of glazing, in sanding the sash carefully, protecting the glass pane from the paper's grains with a fingertip, in the decisions made on each of the window's sixteen panes, something small is set straight that affects the universe. Window glazing requires a dangerous angling of your body if the putty lines are to be drawn straight and true. Everything sits arranged on the sill—hammer, sandpaper, primer, points, and putty. The dissonant parts of yourself hang divided in the graph made by the window sash. To fall inward toward your reflection would be as disastrous as falling backward, to the ground. This tension feels natural, good. The morning smelled of sweat and of the linseed oil rubbed into the wood yesterday to revive its vigor. You feel full of a pith which pleases women.

"I made you some coffee," my mother said one morning. She stood at the ladder's bottom in her robe and slippers. I came down the ladder for the coffee.

"It's going to be a *good* day, isn't it?" A good day meant she would not need crying or the pictures.

"It's going to be a *great* day," I said.

We shared a cigarette. She allowed me to smoke on certain mornings like this. Often she talked to me about the way she felt.

"The problem, Richard, is that everything makes me so sad. It's like Christmas, with all those presents. Most people look at the gifts and think of all the nice things inside. But ever since I was a small girl, I've worried about tearing the wrappers open and finding something inside I didn't want. The wrappers were so pretty, but I was always afraid they were hiding something awful. Is it like that for you? Are you afraid of finding something inside that you don't want?"

I told her that almost anything but long underwear suited me fine.

"You're like your father. You're lucky you're easy to please. Any other man would probably have left me, I know. I get mad at him for *not* leaving, Richard. Then I get mad when he isn't here. Isn't it strange, the way you feel sometimes?"

"It'll be a good day," I said. "Don't worry."

My mother went inside, and I stood for a moment admiring my work and the sun held tightly in the window. The ladder sagged as I climbed back up. As I passed my mother's room, I stopped to watch her in her bathroom before the mirror. She was brushing her hair, and I was startled when her hair held static and a few strands reached up to grab at the brush. She stroked, stopped to scrutinize something in her face, resumed. The awkwardness of being outside and not able to affect her settled in my stomach. She saw me for an instant and waved and went back to her reflection. The wave was one of those waves you see from someone on a porch when he suddenly notices a passing car and gives in to the urge to establish some kind of human contact.

SATURDAY AFTERNOONS my father said things like "See how this chain fits itself into the teeth of the sprocket?" Home from a week's traveling, he tinkered with motorcycles until dusk. He wore khakis and a sleeveless T-shirt. He bought the motorcycles secondhand—usually from someone who had taken a spill—and restored them. When we had renovated one to mint condition, he sold it, and we began renovating another. Frames hung from the garage's rafters like carcasses. When we got a motorcycle whose rider had been killed, we salvaged the parts. My father wouldn't rebuild those particular motorcycles, nor would he sell to a man with a family. He thought motorcycles were too dangerous for any family man besides himself. His favorite customers were men who had just enlisted. He would tell them to be very careful driving to Fort Bragg and would often talk to them about his own service days. He had been a Navy man, had almost reenlisted. Before he closed each deal, he gave the buyer a list of maintenance tips and tune-up instructions that he made him promise to follow.

"And what about you?" one of them asked. "You still ride?" We had just sold a Triumph to a recruit. When the man toyed with the clutch, the machine jerked forward in a spasm.

"No. I don't really ride anymore." My father pointed at me and the house where my mother was emerging with tea. "I can't afford the chance of taking a spill." He considered our midnight rides not really riding but something else entirely.

My mother brought us tea in Mason jars; the man wobbled down the driveway and missed second gear. My parents had argued that morning over the promotion my father was to get after Labor Day. She had said that two months was a long time to wait for someone in her condition.

"Condition?" he had asked.

"I missed my period," she had said.

"Here comes the new mother now," my father said. "Here." He helped her with the tray. He said that she should be careful carrying things, especially with two strong men around who could do things for her. All morning she had basked in my father's unexpected attention. My father set down the tea and cornered her and gave her a hug and a nip at her ear.

"Baby money." He presented her with a wad of cash. "What say I get some fat porterhouses and a bottle of wine. French stuff."

"This isn't a substitute for your being here, you know." Then she seemed to understand that she had spoiled the moment, and she rushed back inside the house.

"Pregnant women," my father said. He gave me a wink.

"Should I put some potatoes on?" my mother called from the kitchen.

"The biggest you've got," my father yelled. He looked down the driveway at something the recruit had dropped. My father went and picked up his handwritten instructions.

"He'll probably forget to put oil in the crankcase, and seize it up," he said as we walked to the backyard. My father poured charcoal briquettes into the grill, and I stacked them into a pyramid. "Stand back," he said, and after dousing the charcoal with lighter fluid, he lit the fire. Leaning against the sides of the garage and the fence, scattered like giant cicada husks, were more motorcycles that my father's hands would set into motion. My father got a sad pleasure from selling mint-condition motorcycles to people who, he feared, would ruin them.

LATE ONE Saturday night we stretched out on a blanket in the backyard. My mother sat at the blanket's edge and swayed to the music playing loudly in the kitchen. Louis Armstrong was ejecting lonesome notes from his horn. A box of light spilled out the door and held a portion of my mother. My father pointed out the constellations and gave them names.

"How about a dance?" he said, and gathered my mother up into his arms. When he dipped her, she giggled and hugged the back of his neck. They were two shadows, keeping cadence to Armstrong's melody. Now and then my father stopped and looked up into the night sky. "We could travel to China, Richard, with that night sky and a little luck." They resumed their sleepy dance, and I thought, If you dug down past the roots and the fossils and the dead, you'd hit another world. The idea that our disturbances were a small part of something as immense as the world was dizzying. Men had walked in space, two years before, floating dangerously out to rope's length and then hauling themselves back, their feet searching for firm footing and balance in a realm where none could be found. This was how we were that summer.

"Do my back and shoulders," my mother said. She had tired of dancing, and she sat where the light verged into shadows and darkness. My father loosened her blouse's top button. He kneaded her muscles and called her his "girl." She rubbed and stretched herself against his hands. Soon she fell asleep, and he carried her up the steps. "How about a ride?" he whispered to me as he stepped inside. When he came back out, he stood in the box of light and stretched. Now he said to me again, "How about a ride?" We pushed his Harley to the driveway's edge, so as not to awaken her. The Harley grumbled and came to life with a kick.

My father coaxed the engine gently through the gears. We slid through the night like a snake through slick growth. My father eased into the turns with a knowing motion. He said once that you never really ride a motorcycle; instead you let it take you where it wants to go. We traveled for several hours, retracing the same tired path. We rode until the darkness eased into a notion that dawn would come. That night we circled wide of our sorrows.

"Here we go, Buck." The home stretch of a quarter of a mile was straight and streetlighted. My father turned off the headlight.

To ride a motorcycle at night is a simple thing: you become one with the darkness. The engine's motion works up through your crotch and settles in your chest. You feel caught up in the exhilaration of blind motion. I wore no helmet, and I had conversations with my father that occurred only in my mind.

I warned my father that my mother was doing the best she could but that he might lose her if he was not careful. I explained that people are different from motorcycles; you can't make them into what you want. I felt giddy being a father to my father. I assured him that we were all doing the best we could. I couldn't tell my father what I had learned that summer—that trying might not be enough. I understood that for a long time my mother had suspected this—that trying might not be enough—and had it been in her power to do so, she would have protected me from this sad knowledge. Instead I told him the biggest thing I knew—that my mother, by being at home safe and sleeping, was somehow giving me shelter from the sadness of motorcycles on a summer night. The two of us rushed into the road ahead like two sleepers riding the back of a dream.

"Hell, let's just ride to China," my father always said at our driveway. He slapped his pants pocket, claiming that with his change and a few bills we could make it. He was very proud of his motorcycle's gas mileage. "We *could* get there." *There* covered all the possibilities of where we might be headed.

SUNDAY MORNING I often joined my parents in their room. My father snored while my mother read romances. Reading comforted her in much the same way that blowing smoke rings at the screen seemed to soothe her. She was trying to hold things together, warding off depression by intoxicating herself with books whose endings were not surprises. She read romance after romance, all of whose white covers pictured forlorn women about to be saved by gentlemen striding confidently out of the background. As she read to me, I watched my father sleep, wondering if she were somehow interpreting his dreams. When he awoke, he scratched his chest and propped himself on a pillow while she gave us a synopsis of this or that book.

"This promising and beautiful young woman is engaged to a doctor. She really loves a poor but honest young butler. He is a servant in the aging doctor's household. It turns out the young butler is the only living heir to a diamond fortune. Mr. Chad-worth, a trusted aide to the dying diamond magnate, is com-manded to find the last living heir. He successfully locates the butler. She and the butler marry and have a happy life."

"Sounds nice," my father said. "I like to hear you tell us sto-ries." He was up and choosing clothes for his suitcase. "Too bad things are often different."

"Too bad, isn't it?" I heard an edge in my mother's voice.

DURING THE week, my mother left the house only at night. We took her car after dark and bought groceries at a grocery store open until ten. My mother drove with the window up, though the air conditioner was broken. She stopped at each in-tersection and then proceeded in screeching spurts. Once past an intersection, she drove slowly, to avoid any possibility of an ac-cident.

We talked on these rides to the store, my mother usually fret-ting over my father's absence.

"Just let him get his promotion," I said.

"I'm not worried," my mother said. "Another baby will make him stay at home, I bet."

I said it probably would.

"Do I ruin things when he's at home?"

"Not that I know of."

"It's been a good few weeks, hasn't it?"

"Very good," I said.

"It's too early for me to start showing. You understand that, don't you?"

Another time, she said, "I hear you on that motorcycle late Saturday nights. Whatever on earth do you do?"

"We just ride."

"Just ride?"

"Yeah. It's like all of us being on the bed when you tell a story. It's like early morning when we share a cigarette while I'm glazing."

THE LAST Saturday of that month, while my mother visited her psychiatrist, my father and I hunted arrowheads. We took his Harley out to a field with a stone outcropping where the Indians had gotten flint for arrowheads. We parked the motorcycle beside a road sign that warned of low-flying airplanes. A mile away an airstrip for crop dusters had been cut from the tobacco fields and a tract of pine. The planes took off slowly and wobbled in low over the fields of tobacco, spraying them and then floating straight upward where the field gave way to the pines. We were far enough away for a lag to occur between the sight of the plane's rising and the sound of the pilot's gunning the motor. In the far distance cars on the interstate we had exited moved at a sleepy speed. My father and I spread out through the field and poked at the earth's raw redness. It had rained that morning, and humidity made the air seem as heavy as the mud on my shoes. We made several passes through the field, our paths slowly coiling to its center. When airplane shadows passed over me, I had the urge to run catch them and jump on them like a magic carpet. My father and I always met under a pine tree left for shade in the years when the field was planted with tobacco and the workers needed a spot to rest from the sun.

My father got excited when he found an unfinished arrowhead. "This old boy sure knew what he was doing." He showed me a tip with one side left unfinished.

"I think we can do it better," he said. He took out his pocket knife with the bone handle. He began pressure-flaking at what some Indian had abandoned three centuries earlier. My father squatted on his hams. His veins grew into a web as he tried to remove the flakes in exactly the right places. Now and then he struck the arrowhead a quick tap. Earlier that morning he had argued with my mother, accusing her of blaming him for things that were beyond his control. My father's knife *tick-tick-ticked,* and he seemed a child again, fumbling to make something whose exact shape he was still trying to discover.

INSTEAD OF a promotion they gave my father responsibility for half the state of Tennessee. This meant he would be gone even more. The whole Saturday morning of Labor Day weekend he refused to talk. Instead he cleaned and recleaned his Harley's spark plugs. Then he readjusted their gap. He cranked the engine again and again, listening to the cylinders' compression. Then he attached the plugs and laid them against the casing. He kicked the starter to watch their arc.

"It's my fault," my mother said. She came out from the bedroom to stand behind me where I stood at the kitchen door, watching. She had the box of photographs under her arm and a note in her hand. She told me to give the note to my father. Then she locked herself in the bedroom.

I read the note and then carried it to my father. The note said, "You've been doubting that you love me for some time now. If it's another mouth to feed that you're worried about, don't. I just made the baby up."

"Here," I said. He stuck it in his pocket. He had the plugs back in and was working degreaser into his hands.

"You might want to read it now."

He read it and threw down the rag with which he was cleaning away the loosened grease. When I got into the house, he was banging on the bedroom door.

"For God's sake, open up," my father said.

"Just leave," my mother said. "Love me or leave me, but the way things are now has to stop."

"Why did you claim to be *pregnant?* Just to trick me?"

"Didn't you notice how things changed when you thought I was pregnant?"

"Open up right now," my father said. "You hear me? Open up right this minute."

"I'm not coming out until you calm down," my mother said. "I might not even come out until this afternoon." She started slipping the faceless pictures of herself under the door.

"What in the hell is this supposed to mean?" he asked.

"It's how I feel. Have you spent so much time traveling that you don't understand *that?*"

"I understand one thing—it's time for a change. I'm taking my son with me, and I'm going to get drunk. D-R-U-N-K." He led me from the house to the Harley.

MY FATHER didn't get drunk that night, but by nightfall we had made the Appalachians. My father stopped at a tourist trap named Blowing Rock. It was near a road tunnel that fed through the mountains into Tennessee. We parked by an information sign that told of the legend of Blowing Rock. An Indian maiden jumped, and her lover, returning late from the hunt, saw her fall. He prayed so hard as she tumbled in the wind that God heard, and He blew her back up to the cliff's edge and safety.

"What the hell," my father said. "An Indian Lover's Leap." The sign said that this legend explained why anything thrown off Blowing Rock rose back up. On a windy day it could snow *upward* here.

My father stood near the guardrail and scratched his head. He pulled a cigar from his jacket and licked and puffed at it. He held himself to three a week. "This is the best way to taste a cigar," he said, and I didn't know if he would light it. Finally he did.

"Sometimes I believe she does everything in her power to drive me away. Richard, I never bargained for a crazy woman, even if I *do* love her. The hell of it is, I never once thought it would turn out this way." The cigar glowed and blinked at intervals. "There goes my own business," he said. "Tennessee." He pointed toward the darkness where the mountains, though invisible, could be felt.

"It's not like you've really been home a lot," I said.

"Well, they sure fixed that problem for me, didn't they? I can't work for them after they throw me stinking Tennessee." He looked at me with bewilderment. "Richard, what if your mother and I *can't* make a go of it?"

My father reached into his pockets and gathered his change. With his head making an arc of light, he motioned me to follow. "Let's try this out, Buck." He leaned over the guardrail. He pitched coin after coin off the mountain's edge, leaning as far as he could to watch where they went. We felt no wind that night, and of course they did not rise. After the coins he tried rocks and sticks and even paper cups rummaged from the trash bin. In the moonless night he was a shadow gathering pieces and tossing them off. Each object was sucked from sight as it fell. He stood there, a man tossing things off a mountainside, caught in the human hope that they would rise again as promised. The night was as dark as I imagined the far side of the moon might be. The thought occurred to me that though we could, we wouldn't keep going west; we had gone as far as it was possible to go and still turn back.

My father crushed the cigar near the motorcycle. "Climb aboard, Buck." We drove to the main highway and turned toward home. I thought of how the road leading down from the mountainside was steep and dangerous. Around one bend or another would lie a blind curve whose far side held secret what might or might not be. As we approached that curve there would arise in us a steady drumming. Our chests would swell and throb until our pulse beat in the quicks of our fingertips. We were blood-full of the moment wherein, against all probabilities, you lean into the curve and take your chances of making it. You feel earth-bound, not by the motorcycle but by your urge to round that bend. Oil slick or happy ending, complete with a hero's welcome, you ease into that snake of road whose other side holds your future hidden. This moment is what men love for. You are father and son, caught in a homeward motion.

"Hold on," my father said, and we went at that curve with all the speed and hope that we could muster.

The Woods at the
Back of Our Houses

ALL OUR domesticity has a perimeter of wildness, and when I was fourteen, mine was the woods which began where our neighborhood ended. This was the summer man walked on the moon and my mother walked out. I couldn't stand the empty feeling of a house my mother had quit, or the sound of my father forever hammering on the damaged sportsfisher he had bought when this latest piece of misfortune entered our lives. My father, convinced that my mother would regain her senses and leave her dentist boyfriend, spent his spare time patching up the big boat for her homecoming.

"This baby is destined to round Cape Hatteras," he said certain afternoons when bourbon had assured him things would get better. He claimed he and my mother and I would dock the boat at a cottage—the kind high on stilts—that he would buy in Manteo, where the first English attempt to found a colony in the New World had failed. My father wasn't bothered that his choice of spots to start over was probably jinxed.

"We'll get these rascals floating." He motioned around our

crowded backyard. "Then we'll leave this neighborhood of land-lubbers and head for the coast, where it's hello good times."

We were the only people in our North Carolina neighborhood who owned three wrecked boats—one for each time something had gone astray in my parents' marriage. We had a skiff celebrating my mother's miscarriage and subsequent nervous breakdown, a ski boat honoring the time my father tried to quit drinking, and the sportsfisher. The sportsfisher squatted at that point in the back of small yards where our neighbors plotted vegetable gardens or chained German shepherds. Past that, all our properties gave way to woods whose trees were the huge, fairy tale kind—mostly ancient sycamores and a few great oaks wrapped thickly with kudzu. Any number of old paths led to certain points of interest: a hole excavated (and abandoned) successive summers in search of lost Confederate gold; a pen where a man named Mr. Hans cursed in Dutch as he pitched together roosters to teach them to fight; and a tumbled structure said to have been a slave quarters or a cathouse, depending upon who told the story. On the east the woods were cut short by the Haw River, where some of the backwaters had been dammed to make Jake's All Nite Carp Pond. Here men waiting to hop a freight train to distant places loitered alongside the out-of-work. A few old men fished eternally for a carp with a tag on its tail which would win a grand prize. Women were rumored to have disappeared around the pond, and once, after we had carved hearts and our names in the tops of the tallest trees, I watched with the other boys as the men with grappling hooks unsuccessfully dragged the muddy water for a missing person. All this and the fact that Jake sold cigarettes and bootleg whiskey to minors made the place irresistible.

My best friend that summer was an orphaned boy named William who had three testicles. We were our neighborhood's paperboys and Peeping Toms. Evenings we slipped into the woods and joined other boys out to see the same sights. We watched people pass from window to window as they acted out their evening lives. One boy—a stutterer we called Ba Ba Bobby—fell from a tree and broke his arm as we watched the Turner girls bathe and compare breasts, and the feel of that unmoored summer will always be for me the panicked sensation of holding my breath on dry land to avert catastrophe as he fell past a window where bathers compared secrets. That boy falling, and the queasy feeling of witnessing pieces of people's lives I wished I hadn't: Doyle Scroggins knocking his wife into the cabinets then mounting her on the kitchen table as she moaned in a language as foreign as other people's dreams; Jewel Rainy singing to her retarded daughter as she untangled the girl's hair and wove it into one long braid; and the hard way old man Walker cuddled his dog after he had gotten drunk and beaten it. We were voyeurs reluctant to recognize any part of ourselves in such desperate rooms.

"I swear, Richard, she *knows* we're watching," William said to me. We had gotten rid of the other boys and were at Mrs. Hans's house. The Hans were our customers, and we considered Mrs. Hans our secret possession. We watched Mrs. Hans waltz naked around her living room and stop to examine her beauty in the mantel mirror. I had never seen a naked woman with a tattoo before; once, when I collected for the paper, she had flung open her robe, and I had stared in disbelief at the anchor on her breast. Mr. Hans had shoved her away from the door and explained drunkenly in his accented English that she was a woman who would lay with colored and children for a drink.

"That floozy is putting on a *show* for us, Richard." William handed me the whiskey stolen from my father. Mrs. Hans moved to a music we couldn't hear. Mr. Hans's feet were propped on the couch—he habitually passed out there—and every few moments she would spin his way and dance before him. I had always thought of Holland as an Old World country chock-full of people who doted over tulips and made wooden shoes, where the women wore pointed white caps which made them resemble kind nuns, but Mrs. Hans wasn't like that. Each of her dances ended with her pouring something from the kitchen—usually flour—on her sleeping husband and laughing wildly.

She cut short her dance by pulling down the shade. We waited for her to step onto the back porch and call in the cat. She sang the cat's name and swooped it up and talked to it the way lonesome people do. We were close enough to my home to hear my father hammering at his sadness as she conversed with the cat, first in English, then in Dutch. The ease with which she switched languages made me understand how far she had traveled to inhabit an old sorrow. She had adapted to the customs of a people who were easily duped by love.

MY MOTHER was an extremely nervous and dangerously beautiful woman who had little luck with love. A few times each week she called to question me about our life without her and to complain that Michael Michaels—the dentist she left my father for—wanted her for only one thing. I supposed she meant sex and changed the subject. I rambled about the paper route I shared with William, the sportsfisher, the maid we hired (a lie) to keep the house spotless, and the peanut boiling party my father gave annually at summer's end.

"We're getting along fine," I said. The kitchen was littered with empty sardine tins and half-eaten cans of beans and franks. "We eat out a lot—steaks and shrimp and stuff. We make sure we get in all of the basic food groups."

"Of all the nerve," my mother said. "You throw a party to celebrate something, *not* when your wife leaves you."

"When are you coming back?" I asked. She had had other

boyfriends, but she usually tired of them in a few months. And, she had *never* left home for one of them.

"Oh, Richard, I'm so confused." When she started to cry I hung up.

Once a week I rode my bike some five miles to the far side of the woods where Michael Michaels's subdivision began. I always stopped to sneak a cigarette at the hill on Tucker Street where our neighborhood ended. The power company had cut a four-mile swathe through the woods and erected steel steeples to carry electricity to distant places. I climbed past the DANGER, HIGH VOLTAGE sign and sat on a girder and practiced my smoking. Some of the houses in Michael Michaels's neighborhood had slate roofs, and I wondered what type of noise rain made on them. I got a sense of detachment from looking down on the tops of things. At such a height, the piedmont along the fall line resembled an old, medieval tapestry on which everything people did—eat and drink and sport—was bordered by woods.

I smoked and thought about the time my mother had insisted we play the game she called electricity. I had been eight and she had just gotten back from an institution. She had instructed me to hold her hand in paper doll fashion while I grabbed the hot wire which protected her flower garden from woodchucks. I had stood there being a conductor, feeling nothing while my mother got the shocks. I was full of the discrepancy of being separate from her pain yet connected. My father had come home and caught us at the game, flinging his briefcase full of x-rays taken by the machines he sold. They scattered though the yard like strange seeds which saw through the flesh of things and threatened to take root and expose. He screamed she was a drunk who was trying to make a nut of me too, and then he had grabbed her hand and a metal stake to ground us. We held hands so tightly that my palms perspired, and I understood that here was sweaty proof of how we were connected—safe from shock as long as we stood like that.

This was the woman I was reluctant to visit, and at Michael Michaels's she was sunbathing—something she never did at home. There was a pool, and she tested the temperature before diving in. I was ashamed at not knowing that she could swim.

She asked me was my father drinking too much, did he have a girlfriend yet, was the house in shambles? Once, when she had been gone over a month, I visited when Michael Michaels came home early from work. He walked toward my mother with two tall, sweating glasses. He gave her one and bent to kiss her and pinched her neck.

"Snooks," she said. "That hurt."

"Does it, now?" he said. He turned and sized me up. "Richard," he said. "You don't have to be such a stranger around here." He stuck out his hand, so I gave him my best grip. What did my mother see in this old man who drank gin with her at one in the afternoon and who yanked teeth for a living and whom she called "snooks." He mumbled he had forgotten the limes and went back inside the house.

"Don't you miss me?" my mother asked. Instead of saying *yes, please come back,* I started saying my good-byes. I claimed that, as a paperboy, I had a huge responsibility to deliver the news on time. The big headlines that summer were all about the moon shot; I told her NASA counted on people like me to inform the public about their great effort to put a man on the moon. I explained that I was a small but vital link of a chain which connected every household with the world.

THAT AFTERNOON William and I delivered newspapers as most of the fathers were driving home with their elbows angled out car windows. Even men who didn't know me waved at the part of themselves they recognized. Near the road which fed to the interstate, a traveler flagged me over to buy a paper and ask directions. The way he eased back onto unfamiliar streets made me imagine standing on the interstate with my thumb out. For an instant I fathomed the strength it would take to quit this place. A few customers on the end of the route were eating at their picnic tables to escape the kitchen's heat, and I fought the crazy urge to introduce myself as someone who had decided to join their family. In another yard, three children too young to know better ran naked through a sprinkler. The Warrens' old dog, Trixie, which had lost a hind leg to the garbage truck, was already worrying a trash can set out for the next day's collection. I understood that my mother, by staying with Michael Michaels and becoming a person who could swim and leave us, risked not getting back. I remembered a story my father had told me about John Glenn; my father claimed the man kept falling in the shower after he got back from outer space. Imagine it: a guy gets the water just right and thinks he's in for a good shower; then wham, out go the lights and he wakes up with a knot on his head and his wife leaning over him after she has called the doctor. My father claimed it was all those miles John Glenn traveled catching up with him which made John Glenn faint. What I wondered about, as I threw the last paper, was that instant before John Glenn's fainting spell hit. Did he feel a part of himself come up from behind and pass that man in the shower, did his heart skip a beat, or did he experience the sensation that all travelers feel when, the journey about to begin, you make peace with a part of yourself you have decided to leave behind? Then the empty paper bag parachuted behind me, and I rode hard against its seatbelted feeling.

"At least you got a mother to visit," said William. We had finished delivering papers and decided to spend the night fishing at Jake's. The carp were so often caught that their mouths were a nest of old sores. We fished alongside men who couldn't sleep at night and who mumbled to themselves. Everyone bank-fished with their rods secured in stands. A string of bare bulbs around the pond afforded at best a stark fisherman's light which swung with an evening breeze. The dirt road which encircled the pond allowed people to fish from the hoods of their cars. You bought a ticket to fish at a cinder-block building which doubled as an ill-equipped grocery store and pawnshop. When someone quit the crap game going on inside to bang out the back door and urinate with both hands against the building, the pinball machines inside dinged with the promise of free games. On busy nights Jake sent Marathon—a half-wit who ran in the manner of the retarded with outstretched hands—to collect dollars against a five-buck prize for the biggest fish of the night. Marathon rode an old bike with wire baskets and a bell which he rang like a cash register when someone paid him. He had some albino in him, and all around the pond people rubbed his head for luck.

To fish for anything as worthless as carp is an act of faith. You catch them with doughballs flung as far toward the pond's center as you can manage. Sometimes you land a catfish, potbellied from a diet of dough, and you fry it on the spot. The flesh tastes faintly of the pond's bottom and of unseen things. When a carp hits, the drag sings and the rod bends double. They are not of the class of fish which leap and somersault, but of an older order which hugs the bottom and subsists on detritus. In the water they resemble golden flashes, things come up from the deep to manifest themselves briefly. A scale or two usually gets damaged from the netting and falls off, smooth to the touch, a silver-dollar-sized and translucent coin of passage. If the fish is big enough, you yell for Marathon, who will weigh it. Fishermen come over to inspect your catch and huddle around it. Marathon cradles it like he'd cradle a baby because he hasn't mastered the art of paralyzing a carp with his thumb and medial finger in its eye sockets. You saw a paralyzed woman once, when your father took you to the hospital to visit your mother, and you think about that—a person unable to feel anything. Then you pinch your arm hard to feel yourself hurt. You wonder why your father doesn't go over to Michael Michaels's and slug him and win your mother back.

"Picture?" asked Marathon. He always carried a camera for such occasions. William and I gave him a buck to take our picture. We each held a portion of the fish, and I was suddenly glad my parents were alive and I didn't live with an uncle who put belt marks on me, as William's did. I thought it might be nice to send the picture to my mother, a snapshot of me and my pal William who had, miraculously, three testicles and much trouble, holding a carp between us, not the carp with the tag on its tail, but at least a big carp. It was one of those moments of goodwill which, like the picture, never got delivered.

EVERY TIME that summer my father broke down and called my mother at Michael Michaels's house, we were working on the sportsfisher. The hole we would never adequately repair made the hull look cannon-shot. Two old Evinrudes sat powerfully beside each other on sawhorses with their props in big steel drums. Certain nights my father filled the drums with water and started the engines and smiled at their grumbling. Black oil bubbles surfaced and burst into colors, and he would stare at them as if he could divine them. Soon he'd amble inside and pick up the phone. The big boat had a canvas top we sometimes sat under when a quick rain caught us working late. We'd switch off the motors and the work light and listen to the rain on the canvas and the woods. You could feel people living around you more than you could see them, and most of the houses were dark except for bathroom lights or the paleness of a room where a hus-

band lay sleeping in front of a television. Now and then someone came to the back door to study what they could see of the
weather, and at the first mention of lightning our nearest neighbor would scream for her kids to get out of the bath. Rain on
canvas made me feel shipwrecked, but it reminded my father of
my mother.

"Excuse me, Richard," he'd say, and trudge to the house. He
walked with his hands in his pockets and his head bent against
the weather. I left him alone to call my mother, because I didn't
want to hear him beg. He always came back pretending he'd
gone inside for a cold beer, and the festive swish saddened me as
he handed me an opened can. He explained I should watch out
for the stuff—it could get the best of anyone, he said—and I
never knew if he were talking about drinking or about what had
transpired on the phone. When the rain quit, we'd work and
talk.

"When your mother comes to her senses, Richard, you'll have
to help her put this summer behind her. What we'll do is move
to Manteo, like colonists, and start things over."

"Those guys got lost," I pointed out. "Why in the hell do you
think they call it the Lost Colony? Besides, we're never going to
move to Manteo." I had gotten tired of his crazy dreams.

"*You've* got to put this behind you, Richard." Then my father
patted the sportsfisher's hull. "We've rounded the cape once before, and when we get this baby in shape, we'll do it again."

Rounding Cape Hatteras was my father's way of reminding
me that we were hewn from tough stock. In better times, my father and I had once chartered a boat to troll for king mackerel
past the shoals. The sea had been so rough that day that even the
captain had taken a healthy swig of my father's whiskey. I listened
to my father sand the sportsfisher's hull, remembering how we
had safely crossed rough water. The diesel had rumbled solidly

beneath the cypress decking as my father and I had found our sea legs and the mate had set out the lines. My father believed we could do it again—power through all those whitecaps and laugh at where we had been.

AFTER SEVERAL days of hard drinking, my father decided to throw his peanut-boiling party early to celebrate man landing on the moon. He felt connected with the space program because the x-ray manufacturer which employed him made a vacuum tube used by NASA. He bought fifty-pound burlap sacks full of peanuts and got out the big kettles. He strung his boats with colored Christmas lights and lettered a banner which proclaimed THE MOON IS OURS! William and I rolled invitations inside the newspapers and delivered them to the entire neighborhood. My father spent the day of the party running errands and buying things we couldn't afford. Some checks had been bouncing lately, and I mentioned this when he came home with a hundred-and-fifty-pound half hog.

"*I'm* running this show." My father claimed it was uncouth to eat boiled peanuts without barbeque. The hog would only fit in the bathtub, so that's where we put it, and my father rushed off to buy ice while I started digging the pit. While he was gone, my mother called.

"Richard," she said. "This bastard won't let me leave. He's holding me captive here." Her voice sounded drunk and crazy and strained. "Put your father on the phone. I *need* him."

"*Lady.*" I tried to talk in a stranger's voice. "You've dialed the wrong number. The family who lived here moved." I hung up and took the phone off the hook.

William and I greeted the guests and showed them the back-yard, where my father had positioned as many TV sets as his credit card could muster. From any point in our yard, you could see at least one set which would broadcast man walking on the moon. Of the hundred and fifty people invited, only fifteen came, and those were already drunk. I had been a Peeping Tom on several of them, and I felt odd inviting them into my own yard and my own calamity, especially Mrs. Hans. She came in an ill-fitted party dress designed for an Old World occasion. The thing had an apron. William complimented her on her attire. She had crooked lipstick, and she had forgotten we were her paperboys.

"I live on the next street," she said. "I have sore feet from these slippers and from walking here." She took off her shoes and handed them to me. "I am sorry I am late." She wobbled toward the drink table. Mr. Hans arrived huffing shortly afterward. He claimed they had been at a party in another neighborhood—he showed us a bottle of champagne they were *giving* away—where he had misplaced his wife.

"Here's her shoes." Then I pointed toward Mrs. Hans apologizing to a group of men, claiming she was sorry she was late. Mr. Hans stuck the fancy slippers in his pockets with the heels pointing out. He seemed about to say something—I guessed it might be about his wife—but he thought better of it, and he shrugged. He seemed suddenly both a foreigner and a kinsman. I wanted to ask Mr. Hans, who had been pulled here nearly four hundred years after the Lost Colonists and the first settlers, if he could remember his first glimpse of what was once called the New World? Did it take his breath, was it like rounding the cape and gauging where you were going by where you had been, did he hug his wife tightly and point toward the life he imagined somewhere past the circling seagulls? All that traveling, based on something as unfounded as a hunch that life would improve where there was space enough to start over, all that traveling to land here in this small backyard filled with wrecked boats and people who had not been invited to other parties or who had no place to go. Suddenly, my father's party seemed a sad celebration attended by people who had missed the holiday.

BY MIDNIGHT, the revelers had stormed the house and found the stereo and records my mother had left. They played Lady Day so loudly she filled the backyard. Mr. Hans was drunk and had lost his wife again. He looked for her under chairs and in the trailered boats; then he sat back in the dewy grass and passed out. I peeped in the kitchen window and watched a neighbor answer our phone and explain his presence. At the far end of the yard, my father was showing his boats to a man caressing the back of a woman who wasn't his wife. Walter Cronkite was excited because the guys had landed on the moon and would walk soon. He described the complicated suits the astronauts would wear to sustain life in a hostile realm. When my father started telling anyone who would listen of his navy days during the Korean conflict, when he had shot the big guns from the destroyer at the enemy, William and I decided to sneak to the carp pond with some commandeered whiskey. My father kept explaining that their target had been invisible below the horizon.

AT THE carp pond, we met up with Ba Ba Bobby who said that he'd swap some of the whiskey we waved for a treat we'd never forget.

"We don't feel like looking into people's houses tonight," I said.

"I'm not talking about *looking.*" He scratched under the arm of his cast. "I got me a gold mine tonight," he claimed. "Come on, now."

We followed him through the woods along the old path which smelled damply of dew and forgotten places. William cursed at a spiderweb and threatened Ba Ba Bobby that this better be good. We circled back through the woody darkness of where we lived. The noise from my father's party came in waves as someone fiddled with the stereo's volume or as laughter from an old joke grew and subsided. The stolen whiskey made me slow to understand our whereabouts.

"Look." Ba Ba Bobby giggled. "She's drunk so much whiskey she don't know who she is." He hooked both thumbs in his belt loops. "I've already had her twice, with her begging for more of me and more whiskey."

Mrs. Hans had taken a sheet from her clothesline, and she sat cross-legged in its middle. She was naked. She asked Bobby had he brought what she had requested; I didn't know whether she meant us or the liquor. William rubbed his hands together at our great, good luck. We lounged beside her like three boys at a picnic who were not in the midst of a naked lady. We passed the bottle around like old chums. I worried about Mr. Hans, until William reminded me that he was passed out in my backyard. Between slugs of whiskey, Mrs. Hans allowed us to grope her and fondle her breasts. She gave us wet kisses and tickled my brain with her tongue in my ear. She said she had taught Bobby something special which he would now show us, and when he pulled his face away, I took my turn putting my face there too.

"We will now screw like dogs," Mrs. Hans said. She growled and barked and was very much out of control. I unzippered and massaged my erect awkwardness until my turn. Strangely, she wouldn't allow us to enter her until we murmured we loved her—as if that phrase magically righted our actions. By my turn she seemed hungry enough to devour me, but seconds later I didn't care; let her do what she would with me, as long as I could journey into that sensation again. I had never come with anyone before, and when I did, I felt jettisoned. We practiced grappling with love and other newfound feelings under a fat moon where men were walking. It's strange, the way you learn to wear the weight of such moments.

BACK HOME, my mother's car sat in the driveway. I eased around the corner of the house like some stranger returning to peek in on his own past. My father was explaining to my mother what she had missed—over a hundred people at his moon-walking party! My mother said that Michael Michaels had taken advantage of her, that she'd just come back to get some things she'd forgotten, but that she was tired and needed a place to rest for the night. My father mixed her another big drink, and she laughed when he pointed at two drunks asleep in the grass. One was Mr. Hans, and I felt not guilt but relief. When "Strange Fruit" came on the stereo, my father asked her for one last dance. I wondered how many more drunken nights this could continue.

When my father saw me, he twirled my mother and said, "Look who's back." He gave me a look which said he knew it was only for a few nights, but that I should accept it. This unwillingness to let go was all we had left of one another. We seemed three Lost Colonists, waiting for a boat with provisions which would arrive too late. I thought about how those colonists had been forced to quit their bickering and to wander inland and lose themselves amidst a wilderness. More successful colonists would follow, towns would get built, towns with neighborhoods and lives like the ones we were quitting. What would one of those early colonists think if he were to wander from the woody dream of lost times and witness my parents dancing the way people dance when they know the night is over, but they are reluctant to allow it to end?

"Hey," my father said when the song had passed. "What we all need here are some freshly boiled peanuts." He promised there was nothing in the world boiled peanuts couldn't fix. The other guests had carted off whole joints of barbeque, and I suspected he was trying to hide the fact that he had little else to offer. "I stashed an untouched sack in the closet, so these hungry bums couldn't get at them."

My mother said for us both to stay put; she'd boil them on the stove in a jiffy as the fires had gone out. My father said that by God we'd christen the sportsfisher by eating them in it. My mother went inside, and my father and I shared a beer and the good feeling of one of the last suppers we would all ever eat together. When my mother returned with a platter of peanuts, we climbed into the boat, and I stared at the strong back of this strange man who could welcome disaster back into his life as if she were a goddess in disguise.

Is that what happens when your childhood quits on you and you are face-to-face with your luck as an adult, full of that queasy feeling which comes from too easily accepting the strange slipperiness of following where others have already traveled? I sat amazed at the type of person I was becoming—one who had taken advantage of a drunken woman but who didn't feel guilty enough to confess. How had events become too complicated to unravel from intentions? I sat there that night with my mother and father in the trailered sportsfisher, reluctant to go anywhere, hungry for a meal as simple as salted, boiled peanuts with these people who had already gone their separate ways. Out in the woods at the back of all our houses some cats were wrangling.

"Listen to them go at it," said my mother. Those cats caterwauling seemed the oldest noise in the world. The darkness became suddenly frightening as we sat listening for something friendly to save and to remember. We lumbered out of the sportsfisher only after my father remarked that it was already the next day and time for bed.

"I got an idea," said my father. "Let's walk like those guys on the moon." He had taken our hands, and together we imitated the movements of people who weren't afraid to test space. My father said we should walk more stiffly—after all, he said, we were in a place where gravity was lessened. It was like stumbling through a dark room whose furniture had been rearranged, and where each moment you dreaded the shock of striking something new.

At the Edge
of the New World

How do you begin to judge your father? The Coast Guard and the insurance company investigators would list my father as blameless in the boating death of Lamar Locklear, our next-door neighbor and my father's business partner. The boat— a sportsfisher—was christened the *Nell*, a name my divorced parents had chosen for me had I been born a girl. My father and Lamar considered the *Nell* firm evidence that, when I finished college and married Lamar's daughter, Holly, and joined their electrical wiring company, we would all be well underway toward something better than our backlashed lives along the Haw River in North Carolina. We couldn't afford to berth the sportsfisher, so the *Nell* rode out snowstorms and summer cloudbursts on a trailer which straddled a drainage ditch dug as a property line. Then, when hurricane season lowered the coastal rental rates, we hauled the sportsfisher to Hatteras Island, where each year we vacationed at a sound-side cottage, complete with a widow's walk my mother had waved from in happier times, before my parents' divorce. A breezeway which reeked of creosote connected our cottage to an identical one that our fathers rented for prospective clients.

My father and Lamar were happiest these two weeks of each year, especially at dusk, when the cottage smelled of bacon-wrapped mackerel steaks and Old Bay–seasoned water set to boil, clattering with crabs from our trap. Each evening, when the lighted mainland across Roanoke Sound seemed a piece of the night and stars poured down, my father and Lamar made a ceremony of lighting their boat.

"No more arguments or complaints," my father always said. "The Italian has passed over." It was one of his favorite expressions—the code words to the Allies that the A-bomb had exploded. Lamar then plugged in a drop cord strung from the cottage to the rickety dock where the *Nell* was moored, illuminating its outline with Christmas lights. My father and Lamar each threw an arm around the other's shoulders and hefted their Seven and Sevens: they had escorted us across the sound to a land of latticed cottages built on stilts, to a world where executives and senators summered and where the first English attempt to found a colony in the New World had failed. My father and Lamar were determined their beachhead would not give or falter.

The night the Lucases were due to arrive, we gathered in the kitchen after the ceremonial lighting, and my father toasted, "Here's to the Lucas deal." Frank Lucas was a purchasing agent from Southern Bell. He and his wife had been invited to the island for a fishing trip, and they would be staying in the adjacent cottage. Lamar had bid on the wiring for a new Southern Bell plant which would house satellite construction. Up to that point, most of our company's jobs had involved houses or restaurants, and were very earthbound.

"Here's to the big executives," Lamar's wife, Wanda, said. "Ha." She sank into a wicker chair in her housecoat with her knees at angles against the armrests. "You call renting this cottage during hurricane season a damned vacation? Holly, you take note of this. Richard," she said to me, "you, too. I could have married anyone, but who did I pick?" Around the kitchen were cans Wanda had opened and left sitting. Wanda Locklear opened cans when she got drunk and angry.

"Our ship will come in," promised Lamar.

"It already has." Wanda pointed to the sportsfisher strung with lights like a celebration no one had bothered to attend. She was an LPN, hooked on gin and codeine, who got cranky when we limited her supply. Holly helped her mother to the bedroom to ready themselves for the Lucases. I slipped in after them while Holly combed her mother's hair. After Wanda promised not to manufacture a disturbance that night, Holly fed her a pill from the supply she governed.

On the mainland, once or twice each year, Wanda wouldn't come home from work, turning up usually at an interstate motel or, once, drunk and naked in the back of her sedan at an all-night carp-fishing pond. When the police brought Wanda home on these occasions, Lamar would meet the squad car at the edge of our shared driveway, wearing Wanda's housecoat over his underwear and seeming much older than his forty-five years.

"You're a bastard," Wanda would scream at Lamar and the sleeping neighborhood. "I want everyone to know you've made me into what I am." Money would be passed so her name wouldn't appear in the newspaper. Soon she would sob she had done nothing wrong—she had just gone out for a little fun, and now everyone thought the worst of her. Once, after the police left, Lamar struck her so hard she lost an incisor. Wife beating and noisy front-yard battles were part of our world. Lamar took Wanda inside and put her to sleep. Then he ambled back outside and unchained his German shepherd, Lucky, who slept beneath the raised bow of the *Nell*. As he dragged the dog to a drum filled with used motor oil, its splayed paws cut sharp lines in the dirt.

The dog had a perpetual spot of mange on its flanks, and old motor oil was thought to be a home remedy for the disease. Lamar always lifted the mutt by grabbing handfuls of flesh along the withers and rump, so that its muzzle was stretched into a grin. Again and again he dunked the German shepherd as it howled. Upon release, the dog shook and rolled in the drainage ditch. As if in need of regaining its master's good graces, Lucky brought a stick to Lamar, and they played fetch at first light, while down by the Haw River you could hear the mill generator's high-pitched whine as it struggled to convert water into a substance as ethereal as electricity. I watched them from my bedroom window, convinced that their sorrow would never be my own. Like most people, I actually believed I could escape where I came from.

THE LUCASES were a mismatched couple who warred openly. They brought their clothes to the cottage in steamer trunks like refugees. Frank Lucas kept asking why we hadn't invited a swatch of local residents and a senator or two to celebrate his arrival. My father, embarrassed that as renters we knew no one here, blamed the lack of revelers on the stormy Coast Guard forecast. During cocktails, Frank Lucas launched into his life story. Two tall drinks later, his North Carolina rags-to-riches account had exhausted itself. On the third drink, he wanted to arm-wrestle "Mister College." He beat me twice, though I tried until my molars ached to slam his arm to the table.

"You've been pushing too many pencils and not enough iron," he said. He was very proud he had risen to purchasing agent without a college education. "Look at what all I got." He flexed his bicep and pointed to the balcony, where the woman he alternately called "Cheri" and "wife number two" shook her hair back and laughed at something Wanda or Holly had said. Cheri was closer to Holly's age than her husband's, and a foot taller, and she wore her boredom as beautifully as any negligee. She and Wanda had struck up the quick, intense, suspicious type of friendship of people who have excesses in common. They discussed which pills to mix with others, and exact proportions. As the women wandered onto the patio, Frank Lucas claimed he golfed weekly with the governor—a man he knew dirt on.

"Now *that's* power," he said.

"You're doing fine," my father said. "You're living the sweet life."

"Damned right." Frank Lucas thumbed his barrel chest and crunched on a pretzel as he splashed out the last of the drink he was waving. "I can make you or break you."

"You up for king mackerel fishing tomorrow?" Any hint of a business deal collapsing made my father skittish. "I bet you've caught trophy kingfish before."

"I've hauled in tarpon and marlin." Frank Lucas imitated a man setting a hook. "Now *there's* two game fish for you."

"You'll like king mackerel," my father assured him. "They fight like hell."

"*I* fight like hell." Then Frank Lucas went to the bathroom.

"This guy's a jerk," said Lamar. "What does he mean, make us or break us?"

"He's just an obnoxious drunk," said my father. "I bet he throws up all day tomorrow while we fish."

"Hey, bub, where's my drink?" Frank Lucas yelled from the bathroom.

"Take him a damned drink," my father said to me.

"Let him get it." I was not taking him a drink while he pissed.

"Let him stick it up his ass," whispered Lamar as the women meandered inside.

"I've got Frankie-boy his drink," said Cheri Lucas. "He likes to bellow a little and blow up after he's had whiskey." She winked at Wanda. "But he's really harmless." She smiled openly at Lamar. "You're part Indian, right?"

"One-quarter Lumbee," said Lamar. "Don't know how the other three quarters got here."

"That's priceless. I've heard Indians are big savages."

"I don't like what's going on here," said Frank Lucas, coming back into the room.

"You don't have to like it." Cheri let her eyes linger on Lamar where they wanted.

"Hey, bub. You flirting with my wife?" Frank Lucas got between Lamar and Cheri. "No one flirts with my wife unless I let them."

"No one is flirting with anyone," said my father. "Hey, we're all friends here. We're all having a few drinks and a nice time."

"That's right, Frank," Cheri said. "No one is flirting here because you don't want them to, and besides, we're all friends." Then she walked over and threw her arm around Wanda, who smiled at everyone from the safe place the pills had carried her. "We were talking origins, Frank. I was remarking about the Indian in Lamar."

"I'm part Lumbee," said Lamar again. "The Indians who took in the Lost Colonists." According to legend, the ill-fated first colonists had searched for gold and bickered instead of planting crops and securing their precarious position at Manteo. When winter arrived without Sir Walter Raleigh's supply ships, they were either killed in a surprise Indian attack or forced to wander inland and lose themselves amidst whatever grace a wilderness had to offer.

"I've got conquistador blood in me," Frank Lucas said. "I got a coat of arms to prove it."

Cheri Lucas rolled her eyes. "Frank sunk a reasonable fortune into a trace-your-family-tree deal. They give you lists of famous people—Louis XIV, George Washington, you know. Frank chose Hernando Cortex."

"Cortés, damn it."

"Cortex, Cortés, whatever. Frank's choices were limited because he's a strict *Catholic.*" She relished the word's hard *c's.* "Catholics never divorce themselves from their past."

Frank Lucas gave her a look that warned this was not the time for this.

"You," she said to my father. "How did you get here?"

"By Buick LeSabre," he said.

"That's *rich,*" Cheri said. My father rarely got a joke, so to hide this fact he laughed hardest. This moment of goodwill uncoiled when Cheri suggested they all get raving drunk and have a toga party aboard the *Nell.* Frank Lucas was quick to produce a camera after they had all changed into bedsheets and Wanda had remarked that a crazy moment like this needed saving. He adjusted the fancy Instamatic on a tripod and fine-tuned the lens and set the timer. Then he grouped us family-style in front of a wide net with cork buoys and dried starfish decorating a wall. As the bulb flashed, I remembered being a kid thumbing through our photo album thick with people left behind from all the new beginnings my parents had launched their hopes upon. Then the feeling passed, and I took my place with the others as we waited for the picture of our new lives to develop.

THAT NIGHT while everyone else toured the sound, Holly and I made love in our room, which adjoined the widow's walk. Discarded furniture salvaged from a yard sale or the attic of the owner's inland home gave the room the temporary feel of a place you visit but never fully inhabit. A salty breeze curved the curtain of the storm door. I stripped and lay naked and proud on top of the covers, smoking a joint to the distant collapse of waves as Holly drew her bathwater. While the tub filled, she smoked a little with me and giggled when she coughed. Standing up, she stretched and slowly undressed, allowing me to explore the parts of herself untouched by the sun. Next she sat before the mirror, combing and twisting her hair into a bun. She clenched the hairpins with her mouth and set into place the coil I would pull down. Finished, she appraised herself in the mirror and checked her teeth. *There will be no hurrying this,* I thought as she touched up the nail polish on her toes and swung around and blew them dry at me. Holly was most beautiful, women are most beautiful, when caught in the purposeful act of readying the gift of themselves for you. They sense in their preparations the enormousness of simple things—the hair held with the exact number of pins needed to fall when pulled free, or the nails painted bordello-red because she appreciates the fact that you like them that way. As she bathed I thought of her before the mirror, and we seemed in no way connected to our parents out squabbling over spilled drinks and lewd passes and which star to mark a course by. First love is that much of a happy conspiracy.

"Don't smoke so much of that stuff that you go sullen on me." Holly toweled herself in the doorway. Too much pot carried me to a place from which only sufficient sleep could retrieve me. Holly led me onto the widow's walk. She kneaded my shoulders and soothed me with easy questions: Were summer school classes hard? (Yes, I answered, but I had passed them.) Did I think the Lucases were a sad couple? (No sadder than our parents.) How soon after graduation would we marry? (We would decide that my senior year.) Did I feel our engagement was constraining us?

"What do you mean?" I asked.

"Do you miss seeing other women?"

"No," I lied. Certain weekends when Holly didn't drive up to Chapel Hill, I slept with a sorority girl named Lisa McQueen, whom everyone called Queenie.

"I wouldn't like to share you with anyone," Holly said.

"Do *you* feel constrained? Is Ron Ramsey still lit up with love for you?" Ron Ramsey was an apprentice electrician with a stutter and a crush on Holly. She worked as a receptionist-secretary for our fathers' business, and once, to demonstrate his love for her, he had unscrewed a sixty-watt bulb, stuck his finger in the socket, and smiled at the bulb's flickering while his body conducted the current.

"He's nothing for you to worry about." When she turned me around, we helped ourselves to each other. A previous vacationer had abandoned a lawn chair, and we tested all the positions its unfolding would allow. The weavings made adhesive noises as we shifted through love. By the time we had both finished, we had moved back inside to watch our joining in front of the mirror. We stood like that until we re-inhabited ourselves and became embarrassed. Then we stretched on the bed to spoon.

"You *do* understand we don't have to know everything about each other, don't you?" Holly had pushed my head into the secure place between her breasts, and instantly I feared she suspected my whole affair with Lisa McQueen. Then I remembered that, before smoking pot, I had told her the story of a college pal and his girlfriend. My pal's girlfriend had walked into his dorm room one morning with a travel bag full of dresses. She asked him which one he liked. After the shade went down, she tried them all on for him. She danced around in a front-buttoning dress like country girls wear, a miniskirt which barely hid the sweet cleft of her buttocks, an evening gown with slits up the sides, and a shift so loose he crawled under it like a kid. Between each modeling, they made a regular feast of their love. She had even brought over the ingredients for mimosas. "I want to dress for *you* today," this woman had said. "Choose." My friend told her the miniskirt made him want to bay like a dog. He even howled a few times—hell, he had been drinking champagne and making morning love. Spring break was the next day, and they were traveling to different places, so they stocked up on the way that skirt made them feel. When school resumed, she confessed she had worn his choice to the abortion clinic. Though my friend didn't want the baby—he was pre-med and his life was on a certain schedule—he broke up with the girl. When he got drunk, he'd repeat the anecdote, as if it meant something whose message he had yet to divine. This was the story I had told Holly earlier. Now, I pulled my head from her breasts and aligned my eyes with hers.

"Are you pregnant?" I asked. "Did you stop taking the pill?"

"Nope." She thumped my head. "I was thinking about how that girl should never have told him about the abortion. It was something he didn't need to know."

"They should have discussed it together," I said. "They should have talked things out."

Holly started laughing.

"What's so funny?"

"When she came over with those dresses, she had already decided to go through with the abortion."

"But wasn't she dishonest?"

"Oh, Richard. That woman *wanted* him to leave her. By telling him what she had done, she was showing him the way out. Come here," and Holly smiled as she guided my dick back inside her. Downstairs everyone had returned; ice was cracked for drinks, and glasses were filled, but we didn't stop, even when I heard someone climb the steps. I could feel them out in the hall, watching. Then whoever it was seemed to understand what was going on in the room, and they shut the door gently, as if we were feverish but sleeping children whose dreams they were hesitant to disturb.

THE NEXT morning, when the sun shaped the offshore clouds into brooding continents, I readied the *Nell* while Holly rowed

Wanda and Cheri a few hundred yards into the sound and anchored our old skiff for flounder. I oiled the big Penn reels and changed steel leaders on the Russel lures. Anything that might heave or toss got battened down. I packed the long coolers with block ice my father had bought before rousting me. Then I chipped two blocks for mixed drinks and iced down the beer. We had gathered two bushel baskets of out-of-season oysters the day before, and I shucked them after enjoying the first few's salty freshness. In the distance a workman hammered at the first of several weekend attempts to winterize his cottage, while out in the sound the women laughed about something.

Much of my adolescence was spent rebuilding that skiff or larger boats, for when anything went wrong in our lives, my father became a renovator. We replaced keels, fiberglassed hulls, covered seats with Naugahyde, and stitched canvas covers to shield us from the elements. Watching Holly and Wanda and Cheri fish, I was reminded of earlier vacations with the Locklears in rented cinder-block bungalows we could barely afford. Somehow, we seemed happy with the cold tile floors and two-burner gas stoves. These places smelled of homemade oil-and-vinegar suntan lotion and leaking air conditioners and the peculiar odor of previous tenants' lives. A tube of discarded lipstick rounded by some woman's lips and hidden in the back of the medicine cabinet confirmed my simpleminded suspicions that others had passed through these rooms, too. Nights, Holly and I peeked from the room with bunk beds we shared. Like cousins, we were pajama-ed and giggling. Our parents danced slowly in the kitchen. Their inland, quarreling existences had been left behind. We slept to their laughter as they played rook or poker or some all-night board game of chance.

Some people reel backward through time when they smell woodsmoke while children build snowmen, others go giddy over a field of summer fireflies, but I am reduced to a blob of sentiment by *Paralichthys dentatus*—the common summer flounder. They still seem strange, flat fish left over from fossilized times. We hooked them at the edge of sandbars with a piece of the first-caught flounder's belly cut into finger-sized strips to imitate a minnow.

When my parents were still married, my mother fished along-side Holly and Wanda. I was nine or ten the first time I saw her fish. Kerchiefed, she sat like a man with her feet apart on the gun-nel. How had she learned to unhook a flounder so quickly or so easily? Because of her nervous lapses into hospitals and other men's many-bedroomed houses, she had always seemed the ghost of my childhood—moody, seasonal, a creature of shut doors and unexplained absences—but when she fished for flounder, I un-derstood my father's love for her. Each time she hooked one, the rod curved into a smile and the line sang. She cursed if the fish bit the leader, then giggled with Wanda like schoolgirls at naugh-tiness. Wanda would be braiding Holly's hair, and my mother would mix gin-and-tonics while my father and Lamar yelled to row in, the carburetor was fixed and the *Nell* was seaworthy. *What do they see in that damned boat?* Wanda or my mother would remark. I would pull hard at the oars and practice my oarsman-ship. On the way in, the talk would shift to how deliciously bo-hemian it was to play cards all night and dance at dawn, and then drink tonics at nine in the morning.

"It's times like this that I wish your mother hadn't jumped ship on us," my father said, boarding the *Nell*. He handed me the shrimp he'd boiled in the cottage. I tossed them in the cardboard box as he poured on the seasonings. We would eat oysters and shrimp all the way to the fishing grounds. He looked at his watch—wishing we were offshore by now—then tuned the shortwave radio. A song on a distant channel mixed with the Coast Guard warnings of moderate to high seas. As my father lis-tened, his face wore the same look as when he talked to my mother with the special telephone extension he had wired from his bedroom window to the fighting chair aboard the trailered *Nell*. She still owned a share of the business, and he consulted her like an oracle. He gave her counsel on her boyfriends and listened patiently to her confessions. The fact that he couldn't have her made her maddeningly desirable. Both my parents loved the Titanic quality of their love. My mother had called just before this vacation to say she was flying to England with some chiropractor. "Don't let your father screw up this business deal," she had said to me. "You don't know the trouble I went through to set this thing up."

My father pitched me a clean bandanna, which I tied on my head pirate-style as he had taught me. "Piece of advice, Richard," he said out of the blue. "Be careful what you wish for—it might come true." Absently, he picked through the shrimp and ate some small ones, shell and all. Out in the sound, Holly yelled and held up a doormat-sized flounder she had caught. My father laughed and bellowed to quit scaring the fish and get busy catching more. He watched them for a long time, then he turned to me. He had been trying to get his bandanna just right, but the little flap of triangle kept missing the knot. I fixed it for him. I could tell my fingers on the back of his head gave him barbershop memories of when my mother kept our hair cut. He had even bought her a barber's chair at an auction in a clumsy attempt to jump-start their marriage. His gift was exactly the wrong thing; even the garbage men refused to lug it away.

THE PREDICTED storm system stalled, and the wind lay. Aside from the bilge pump, the *Nell* performed like a shipwright's fantasy on a maiden voyage. The rough seas would not arrive until late that night, and the ocean was like a sheet of plastic connected to the sky by a seamless horizon. I mixed drinks for Frank Lucas and Lamar, and we ate with our hands from the pail of shucked oysters. When my father yelled from the bridge to send him up a few, I carried him a coffee cupful, along with a beer. We were men on water, passing around lemon wedges and Tabasco sauce as we estimated what fortune the day would bring. As first mate, my job entailed keeping Frank Lucas liquored up and happy. I shoved the box of shrimp his way and told him to weigh in. There is a pecking order aboard boats, and he was *last*. When Frank Lucas sucked the heads, too, I almost began to like him. We ate until the last mile buoy, when my father gave the sportsfisher full throttle, and we made what felt like Godspeed with the old Chrysler engine humming on all eight cylinders. We planed at twenty, got a smooth bow spray going, and outdistanced our problems as we sped toward where you must reckon by charts and compasses. When I realized we had long since passed our usual fishing grounds, I gave my father a what's-up look. *Blue water,* he mouthed. *Gulf Stream.* We had never taken the *Nell* this far from shore.

Out where the land fell from sight, I got an inkling of why the old-timers called what they saw the New World. It had something to do with inland feelings and left-behind places. You can't look at a continent from that distance without imagining a life in its interior. Before, the closest I had come to understanding this were certain autumn afternoons, during high school, when Holly and I drove my motorcycle into the Haw River countryside. We sped by old clapboard, two-story houses set back handsomely from the road. The yards were big enough to be mowed by tractors, and entire families raked and burned leaves. Kids jumped over flames when their parents' backs were turned, and brothers dumped on bedsheets full of damp leaves, which sent up smoke signals before igniting. Fathers leaned on rakes and watched another end of summer burning. Holly ran her hand beneath my shirt and fingered my navel as she pressed her breasts into my back. On the straight stretches, the Harley topped eighty as we rocketed into the illusion of the road suddenly ending. I imagined I lived in one of those houses with Holly, that *I* had stopped raking to watch two lovers zoom by. Would I wave at how young I had once been; would I remark that their speed tempted Providence; would I wonder at how far inland I had wandered from such recklessness? That day aboard the *Nell,* I was a young man getting his first glimpse of an old feeling called the New World.

"This is the goddamned life," yelled my father. He motioned me up to the flying bridge. He claimed I should learn a thing or two about navigating; after all, the *Nell* would be mine and Holly's whenever we wanted. I had driven countless times before, even weaving safely through the shoals of Cape Hatteras when he and Lamar were incapacitated, but my father made a production that day of handing over the wheel. He fetched two cold beers and called out headings as I marked the course. We took the *Nell* to blue Gulf Stream water, where big mackerel ran so deep we used downriggers. Whole acres of the ocean's surface boiled with menhaden, and I trolled through them to catch the kingfish feeding on the school's bottom. Whenever the *Nell* felt sluggish, my father snuck below to hand-pump the water the bilge would not siphon.

We filled the boat with big kingfish that Frank Lucas fought. Lamar and my father clubbed and gaffed them, and even when there were two fish on, Frank Lucas got angry if he were not allowed to fight both fish to the boat. We played the part of genial fishing guides, even taking pictures as he proudly displayed the largest. Frank Lucas couldn't get enough of catching mackerel, and a greedy part of himself wouldn't allow us to release any. This was before there were ceilings on the number of fish you could keep, and a part of myself was ashamed that we kept fish beyond

what my father called "a gentleman's limit." Our haul was illegal
by modern standards.

ON THE ride back from fishing, my father sipped whiskey beside me on the bridge and fiddled with the shortwave radio while
I held the *Nell* on course. I hoped that he didn't see me at the
helm as something other than it was. I expected and dreaded a
father-son chat: When would I be ready to learn the subtleties of
bidding? Would Holly and I buy a house near his? Would we give
him one grandchild or seven? When this conversation never happened, I was relieved. *Don't go into business with your father,* my
mother had warned. *Strike out on your own.* This was my last conversation with her, and she had promised to have a drink for us
as she crossed the Atlantic. I had thought it a crude remark, but
sitting there beside my father, I understood she meant it as a
salute, as people at a wake toast a life that has passed. When I
caught my father looking up at the sky and whistling, I remembered today was the day she was flying to England with her chiropractor.

"We'll make the dock right at nightfall," my father said. Behind us, Frank Lucas was tipsy and singing "What Do You Do
with a Drunken Sailor." Lamar led him like a choir director. We
habitually sang that when homeward bound, and my father and
I joined in, too. Then Lamar remembered that on *real* fishing
cruises, you strung up the fish like those little triangular flags at
used car lots. By the time we reached the first mile buoy, the *Nell*
was fringed with mackerel. Lamar even hoisted a small one like
a Jolly Roger on the outrigger. The Christmas lights got hooked
to the generator, and a loose connection made them blink. Fisherman on other boats heading back to port pointed at us and
waved the thumbs-up sign. A few displayed their meager catches.
When another sportsfisher tried to run up a mackerel and it fell
off, there seemed nothing funnier. The gossip on the radio in-

formed us that the other boats had heeded the warnings and not risked blue water.

"Landlubbers." My father clapped me on the back. "Bunch of goddamned featherweights." Then he broke into all the channels and began broadcasting our adventure. The liquor had gotten to him, and he kept explaining that luck must be pushed and tested. My father believed that the day's catch was a fortuitous omen.

WHEN YOU push circumstances beyond normal limits, you risk discovering things you don't want to know. Back at the dock, we called the women down to applaud our catch. Mackerel five deep lined the pier like cord wood. Frank Lucas seemed disappointed when my father explained that no one mounted mackerel. We were shirtless and red from the sun and liquor, and we needed a shave and a bath, but we exuded a *good* sort of frontier feeling. The women sensed and admired this. Holly worked lotion into my shoulders and giggled when the imprint of a quick kiss to my neck disappeared.

"Let's have one hell of a party tonight, mates." Frank Lucas had begun calling us that offshore. "Sex and drugs and rock 'n' roll— isn't that how the song goes?" He called marijuana "hooter" and asked my father and Lamar if they partook.

"I'll try anything once," said my father.

"Righto, mate." Frank Lucas claimed he had pills, too—speed and Quaaludes. "I'm a walking goddamned pharmacy." When he produced a fifty and asked would I take care of the fish, my father said that wasn't necessary.

"Don't insult me," said Frank Lucas. "If I want to give him fifty, I will. Where I come from, it's customary to show your gratitude like this." I felt like a valet as I tucked the bill in my pocket. Frank Lucas strung his arms around my father and Lamar and said it was time to get down to some righteous partying and serious business. They walked up to the cottage with Cheri and Wanda following while the ice in their drinks jingled.

"Cheri's not a bad person, but she's not his wife," said Holly. She explained her mother and Cheri had been drinking all day and confessing. Frank Lucas couldn't get a divorce from his first wife because he and she were strict Catholics. When Holly asked if I could imagine what it must be like to know the person you loved would never marry you, I said I couldn't.

"Just put in an appearance, mix them some drinks, and come upstairs to me," Holly said. "I'll be naked."

I set about cleaning our slaughter. The dock had a fish cleaning station with a spigot and a humming streetlight high on a pole. I worked in the cone of light. The wind had increased, and the sound was whitecapping. The clouds hid the stars and moon and lidded in the darkness. There were so many fish that I scored them vertically and pushed out nuggets of mackerel tenderloin instead of steaking them. This was as wasteful as shooting buffalo for their tongues, but I didn't care. The best part—the cheek meat—I left on the fish. I slung the carcasses out into the dark sound for the crabs. By the time I finished, I had bagged and iced over a hundred pounds of mackerel nuggets.

WHEN I walked into the cottage, I saw that Frank Lucas had made good on his promise. Wanda snored with an open mouth on the couch, while Cheri twirled like a dancer around the living room. She spun my way and kissed me wetly on the cheek. Then she started spinning again like an out-of-kilter gyroscope.

"Whoa, now," said my father. "Which way do these things go?" He held a joint in each hand and seemed genuinely confused. He saw me and announced that I was his son—as if that were an astounding and philosophical statement. "Here." He handed me a joint. "We've never done this together before."

When I took a big lungful, its quality widened my eyes. This was Thai stick—good pot laced with opium. Lamar wobbled from the kitchen with a tray of drinks, looked at Wanda, and gave me hers. Three or four more tokes on the joint made me forget my promise to Holly. I reasoned the wait would make going to her more pleasurable.

"Frank," Cheri said. "You're a bastard, and I'm passing out." She lay down like a tired child on the hard floor and closed her eyes. Frank Lucas gave my father and Lamar a what-can-you-do-with-them look and launched into business. He stroked his chin whiskers and calculated. He seemed neither drunk nor high. How long had he waited for this first scent of the end of a deal? He assured us he had done his homework; without his contract, our company would go under.

"Point number one." He looked at my father. "Your ex-wife owns one quarter of the business. She handles her personal life so sloppily she *could* be persuaded to force you to buy her shares. You can't afford to." He looked at Lamar. "Point number two. My friends on your local police force tell me you've offered bribes on several occasions—not that they ever accepted them." Then he looked at me. "There are all types of fellowships available for an enterprising young man, especially if the governor made a few calls."

"You know dirt on him," I said brashly.

"You're such a bright boy." He looked at Cheri and seemed to falter. "She *is* beautiful, isn't she? It's a shame she's lying there like that. Is there a more comfortable place she could sleep it off? Could you help me carry her? All of you."

Wanda's bedroom was the closest. I followed with the high heels Cheri had kicked off. Without any ceremony, Frank Lucas stripped her. I was so high that it seemed like a dream.

"That's not even his wife," I said to my father and Lamar.

"Bingo, Mister College," said Frank Lucas. "What I need is a little help here. You see, after I'm dead, there's a good chance she'll claim common-law wife rights, and I don't want that. I want everything to go to my real wife and kids. If we could just get some pictures of a little *fake* love here, I'd be grateful. I'm talking snapshots of one of you penetrating her, or, say, in her mouth. Hell, she's so Quaaluded she'd never know the difference. I'd put the pictures in a safety deposit box and will my executor the key. No matter what claims Cheri made, the pictures would invalidate them. My lawyer suggested this." I felt a trickle of pity for his indiscreet scheme until I realized we were all desperate.

"What say, mates?" Frank Lucas produced a doubloon from his pocket, which he claimed his grandfather had given him for luck. He suggested a coin toss to pick the leading man. He left and came back with the Instamatic, and he promised he wouldn't get any face except Cheri's in the picture. We were all shirtless and half-naked as we fumbled with his proposition. Then I felt someone at the door. It was Wanda, stoned. She focused for a moment and comprehended. She had been in rooms like this before—terra incognita—and she didn't like them any more than we did.

"You all are no better than I am," said Wanda. Cheri moaned and moved in her sleep, and from where Wanda stood, it must have seemed the naked woman was a willing participant. "Oh, Lamar," she said. "What will we do now that I think the worst of you, too?" When she shut the door, I realized she had seen Holly and me the previous night, and I was ashamed at this room's difference.

"She won't even remember this happened," promised Frank Lucas. I didn't know if he meant Wanda or Cheri. We stood there, three men fighting the invitation to violate her sleeping beauty. If I had been asked, I do not know if I would have participated in the coin toss. I only stayed long enough to know that Lamar would be in the pictures. He ungirded himself and set about the sordid business at hand. My father looked hard at me—as if about to apologize that our search for the good life had landed us here—and our eyes met for the first time as regretful men. Whole ages passed between us in that moment. Frank Lucas readied the Instamatic, and I remembered that, as a kid, I had believed the way the image developed before my eyes was sheer magic.

"Richard, get the hell out of here," my father said—the last command he gave me that I would ever follow—and as I shut the door, I knew I would never picture any of us the same way again.

Up in our room, I confessed everything to Holly, except Lisa McQueen. I began with my nervousness concerning our proposed marriage and ended with our fathers below us sealing a deal. My heart wanted out of my chest, and I couldn't sit down, nor stop talking. I chain-smoked cigarettes by the widow's walk and said I would *not* join the business. Then I cried the tears of a person who wanted sympathy.

Holly allowed me to cry, then said, "Grow up."

"What do you mean?"

"Everything comes with a price. Do you think I *like* playing secretary to save expenses so you can go to college? Don't you think that *I* worry about our marriage? Whatever my father did, he did for all of us. You're so naïve it's almost endearing. You wouldn't . . ." But she stopped when my father and Lamar staggered outside and began yelling at each other. The widow's walk afforded a box view of their argument. Lamar wanted my father to ride with him to the first mile buoy to air their heads. My father explained the *Nell* was not seaworthy in such rough seas. He screamed, had Lamar drunk so much that he didn't understand the bilge pump was malfunctioning?

"All I'm asking for, mate, is a little pretend love," said Lamar. They laughed as if it were the best joke they had ever heard and

clapped each other on the back. Lamar claimed they would take
a little spin like old times, when they were teenagers who had
dropped off their dates and spent whole nights debating love's
mysteries. My father unmoored the *Nell*, but before he could
hop aboard, Lamar gunned the sportsfisher from the dock. My father jumped up and down and shouted curses, but Lamar kept
going. *I am washing my hands of this foolishness,* he yelled. He motioned the-hell-with-you with both palms and zigzagged back to
the cottage.

"He'll just putter around the sound and probably anchor off
a sandbar and drink until he feels better," I told Holly. "It's like
when he dunks Lucky."

"I hope so," she said. Holly and I watched Lamar ease around
the buoy which marked the channel to Cape Hatteras. The
Christmas lights made the *Nell* resemble an all-night party cruiser
out for an aimless celebration. He sang a drunken sailor's ditty
whose words were lost over the grumbling of the engine. Was he
simply drunk, or was he running from the part of himself he and
my father had traded to close a deal? My father would have no
stomach for electrical wiring after that night. He would sell the
company at a profit, thanks to the bid Frank Lucas would award.
The *Nell* would flounder so close to the shore off Hatteras that
the lights of senators' cottages must have winked at Lamar as he
drowned.

As I stood on the widow's walk with Holly and watched
Lamar leave, I wondered what got rabble like us to this place
billed as an earthly paradise. A people like mine were not
pleasure-fearing Pilgrims, nor the landed aristocracy of the Vir-
ginians who would write the Constitution. We would have never
crossed the ocean in an organized migration. What got *my* ancestors here was any situation in which you decided a change in
geography might cure your plight. As the anchor dropped, all we
would own was queasy stomachs. Once inland, we became what-

ever the new landscape required: reluctant but rum-fortified revolutionary soldiers; willing purveyors of smallpox-infested blankets; traders of horses and human flesh; sharecroppers and tent revivalists and, later, owners of used cars and second mortgages and damaged dreams. I *do* know that whatever feeling Lamar was full of as he drove off—drunkenness or loathing or devil-may-care—fueled the journey from the old world to the new one where Holly and I were standing.

"We will not be like that," she said, and I understood we already were. She looked hard at me, the way a woman does when she is deciding something important. I'm not sure what words could have saved us then. I remembered my father's advice—*Be careful what you wish for*—but it seemed an old man's useless warning.

"Ron Ramsey and I are more than just friends." She let this information sink in. She was giving me a way out. I started to give her tit for tat, but she put her hand over my mouth, as if she had guessed about my dealings with girls like Lisa McQueen and had already forgiven me. We stood like that until she decided whatever it was she was thinking and it felt safe to take her hand away.

Is that what happens when two people find themselves marooned at a new place in each other, wrestling not with angels nor with each other but with the sadness of passages? I marveled at the newly discovered place in myself which could make love on a widow's walk to someone I loved but would leave because a greedy part of myself wanted more. I was still young enough to risk my future without her, but old enough to know that the youngness didn't matter. Suddenly, I was as ashamed of myself as I have ever been, yet oddly, I was elated.

For the first time in my life, I made love as an adult, without innocent explorations and with a desperate, hungry roughness. We cursed and clawed and bit. The knowledge that Holly would allow me to be the one to leave made me want to plunder something as mysteriously familiar as her body. I felt full of what I can only describe as the sorrow of conquest—a feeling my ancestors must have dismissed as second thoughts when the sight of the New World took their breaths, while at their backs tugged home and those parts of themselves travelers must leave behind. There would be no end to the new beginnings this fresh-found part of myself would exact. Now, I ask you, what can you do but hope—like your forefathers—that a course can be charted for a lifetime of moments like that?

Everything Quiet Like Church

THE PRACTICING midwife was inside the house helping my wife Lisa break her water with a quick pinch of a fin-
gernail, and I did not want to watch that. Instead I was outside
with the midwife's sister, who had an eye problem and who
drank beer with me as she spun out her life's story. Like me, she
was along for the ride. She had delivered babies alongside her sister until recently, when an ocular disease which ran in her family had claimed 90 percent of her sight, so this near blindness was
as new to her as my becoming a father. We sat at a card table in
some summer shade which danced a crazy jig whenever a breeze
batted the treetops. My faith in midwifery had first faltered at a
home birth preparation meeting, when one of the sisters had
passed around a frozen placenta in show-and-tell fashion. Normal people do not keep placentas in freezers, and I pointed this
out to my wife. Later, the clear-sighted midwife remarked in
passing that she was a Jehovah's Witness. A quack who prayed as
she administered potions and poultices would *not* deliver my
firstborn. I argued midwifery was something you read about in

Old English manuscripts or the Bible, for Christ's sake. Then I yelled that sane people did not have babies in rented mountain-top stone hunting cottages, no matter how broke they were. Lisa had reminded me that it was *she* who was pregnant; she *would* have her way; and for the first time I felt like an outsider to what our quarrelsome love had given heartbeat.

So this retired midwife named Ruby was mapping out her life for me. She was Opal's—the practicing midwife's—sister. Ruby had been a nurse's aide, a baker, a carnival person, and a woman who rode elephants at the circus—all before retiring at thirty-eight. She could rattle nonstop on a smorgasbord of subjects. She pointed out that what she could see of my little tomato patch needed weeding and remarked that the herbs I had grown for the baby's herbal bath were less than robust. I thought two things: no child of mine would be dipped in such a concoction as they had suggested; and when the time came, I would hurry Lisa to the hospital and away from this hocus-pocus. Let Ruby think she was keeping me from underfoot. I opened us two beers from the cooler and settled in to listen.

Ruby was a black widow in her choice of husbands. Her first was killed in a house trailer explosion when a propane tank ignited. He had been a butcher with hearty appetites and sure, heavy hands. Husband number two was a pastry chef with a quick temper which got him killed one night at a roadhouse. A string of boyfriends and some carnival work followed. Her third marriage was to an animal trainer at the circus where she had learned to ride the elephants. He died of a heart attack, and they all left her childless because she was born without ovaries.

"So you delivered babies because you can't have them." She seemed such bad luck that I reasoned the insult might make her ask me to drive her home.

"No. I delivered babies because the one thing about people is that they are always being born."

I had always imagined midwives as squat women dressed roughly in peasant garb with kerchiefed hair. They would eat porridge or use wooden paddles to pull dark, grainy breads from ovens. Ruby wore short shorts and a halter top and fretted over her appearance. A hat with a colorful sash shaded her face, and now and then her fingers adjusted a cameo necklace. She was used to turning heads. Did she dress herself or did the boyfriend she spoke of help? I imagined him choosing her clothes, saying things like, Ruby, this tight dress sure does you justice. I thought, what an odd thing it must be to need to see yourself, while your lover has the only dependable set of eyes.

Now she was comparing midwifery to elephant riding—something which never would have occurred to me. According to Ruby, you had to guide an elephant with your knees and to believe you could control something that large and potentially dangerous. You had to hush what lay under the loose folds of skin. Though the elephant could sometimes spook and quickly turn on you, the rider must believe it wouldn't. You had to become one with the elephant and soothe it through your knees when some kid in the second row popped a popcorn bag which startled the beast. Her job was to ensure the best elephant walk possible.

"That's what midwives do," Ruby said. "They help control a potentially dangerous situation."

And I truly wanted to believe that she could. Lately, when alone, I'd become shaky and afraid. This could happen anywhere. Certain nights, this feeling drove me from bed. At such times, our house at three in the morning was thick with a darkness which made sleep difficult. While the room took shape, my heart beat like a runner's, and I feared nameless things. If Lisa and I had made love before sleeping, this feeling would worsen. I'd stand by the sink and guzzle coffee cups full of water, not from thirst but because the water pipes moaned pleasantly when adjusted to a certain position. Now and then the old house settled and popped like a joint set back into place. I'd light a cigarette and crack the kitchen window to avoid filling up the house with my loneliness. The cars on the highway at the foot of the mountain had to brake for a curve which sometimes hid deer and the possibility of an accident. My head would fill with a father's worries as I smoked and bothered a bad tooth with my tongue. When the feeling got too cumbersome, I'd bump back a shot of hidden whiskey. Then I'd recite the names of things with an understandable order—the planets in their orbits, the alphabet, the year and make of every car my father had owned. When this haphazard feeling finally eased, I'd quit my watch and peek under the sheets at the shape Lisa and I had created, fearful of awakening her and of having to explain what had driven me through our cottage. When the part of myself which had roamed decided to come back home, I'd press my lips to Lisa's stomach and force a half-remembered hymn toward our baby. Here I was, a person in his own house, feeling like a kid spooked at something as uncertain as the dark.

It was fine by me if this out-of-practice midwife thought she was protecting me from all this.

AN HOUR later, I had been inside a dozen times, only to be driven out weak-kneed each time the crest of a contraction slammed home and Lisa groaned. I had heard barroom stories from husbands whose laboring wives threatened to whack off Old Jake if it ever got too friendly with them again, and I didn't want to hear Lisa say this. The late afternoon shade in which Ruby and I sat had become a lengthy expanse through which I paced. Time was not passing properly; it seemed to have skipped town. Ruby was oblivious to this.

"There are some things we need to talk about." Ruby reached down for a lunch pail like factory workers carry. She lay gauze, iodine, string, scissors, ointments, and a cheesecloth on the card table. The simpleness of the instruments of birth struck me. She kept rummaging deep inside the lunch box. As she searched, she named the herbs I would gather and steep in the cheesecloth. She would boil the scissors and soak the string in alcohol. My job was to catch the baby, tie off the umbilical cord, then cut it. Finally, Ruby set nail polish and clippers on the table.

"What's that for?"

"Why, my nails." Then this woman began giving herself a manicure! She accomplished it by feel, pushing back the cuticles with the tiny file and snipping the nails. With her index finger, she felt for rough edges to feather. She even had a little hand brush and some disinfectant. She cleaned each nail meticulously and painted with steady, determined strokes. Her face had the distant look of a daydreamer. She waved her hands and blew on her fingertips. These seemed hands designed to grasp the back of a lover or to bring to your lips and kiss—not for delivering babies. These fingers would *not* aid in Lisa's parturition, I reasoned. She seemed to sense this.

"I know," she said. "I'm only here for moral support. But it doesn't hurt to have clean hands. Now," and she cocked her head to appraise me with her good eye. "Have you and Lisa discussed what you would do if something were wrong with the baby?"

We had. Once, during breakfast, Lisa had asked what would we do if the baby were born with Down's syndrome or, say, half a brain?

"What a question!" I had yelled.

Later, in bed that night, Lisa had eased to my side of the pillow and wriggled my shoulder. "You'd have to help me smother the baby with a pillow if something were wrong." She let this information sink in. "Make love to me, now."

"What if we hurt the baby?"

"That's an old wives' tale."

"I have a headache," I lied.

"My breasts throb, I feel fat and ugly, you won't make love to me, you don't love me." She rolled over to hug a pillow and face the wall.

"Leave me alone," she said when I touched her there. Then she said, "Don't," and giggled. With my free hand, I admired her greatness. She reached back and felt that I meant business. Soon, I had eased myself inside her, and we established our old and easy rhythms. We set the old brass bed to an ancient sort of talking. Finished, I lay inside of Lisa and wondered what our baby thought of our roughhousing. Would our child think it the noise of love, did its force quicken the fetal heartbeat a few paces faster, what would that child know of love's disturbing decisions?

"There will be nothing wrong with the baby," I told Ruby.

"Good." She inspected her nails. "A father has to have faith."

"I've got faith."

"That's the spirit. Still, you sound nervous."

I brushed away the equal-sized and folded pieces of the beer label I had scratched from the bottle.

"If you're religious, and it would help, then pray. You don't seem much like the religious type, but then I'm not either. That's my sister's department. She prays so much she needs kneepads. I'm very practical about God and praying. God sees to His work, and I see to mine." She laughed heartily at her own joke.

"I'm fairly religious," I lied. This retired midwife was making me nervous. "And I'd like to pray, but I'd like to do it by myself, if you don't mind."

"Suit yourself." She gathered the tools of her trade into the lunch pail and declined my offer to help her inside the house. She cocked her head and took steady steps like someone testing the depth or temperature of water. She had claimed she still had enough vision to see the big picture of things, but the tricky way we distinguish, say, a single tree from a group of them had been taken from her. When she stubbed her sandaled toe on the porch deck, she muttered, "God damned," and I liked this woman. At the back door, she thought of something and turned to stare at me. I wasn't taking any chances on her sight; I went down on my knees and pressed my palms together. "You don't believe in things like midwifery, do you?"

I had closed my eyes and wasn't answering.

"Hell, you don't believe in much of anything. You're a part-time college teacher, right? Mister, I don't think I'd want you to teach me anything." Then she was lost inside what was going on in the house.

And she was right. Lately, I hadn't been good at even the simplest situations. I taught three lousy composition courses at the university where I did graduate work. The salary required that I paint houses in good weather so Lisa and I could meet the bills. Creditors were sending warnings in envelopes marked "Personal and Confidential." Certain evenings, Lisa would watch me water the tomatoes, and for no good reason, she'd burst out crying. Any small occurrence—a flat tire on our old Chevrolet or a phone call from her girlfriend who was living happily in California—would cause us to squabble. More than once, wedding rings cakewalked across the kitchen's linoleum.

"I'm getting out of here," I'd yell.

"Why bother coming back," she'd scream.

I always flung a good spray of gravel and made the rocks ricochet against the car's undercarriage as I wove down the mountain. I'd hit every pothole and smile at the muffler's scraping. I'd yell out the window things like: "Who needs this!" If the fight were bad enough, I'd drive thirty miles from Arkansas to Oklahoma just to see the hills quit and the land stretch as flat and unbroken as a promise. At the Welcome to Oklahoma station, I'd pull off and collect free brochures like any other tourist. Once, a few travelers asked me to work their camera and take snapshots of them. They chattered of destinations and portions of inter-states filled with construction. I wished these strangers a safe journey and headed for home.

Near our house, I always stopped at a pizza place and ordered a large pepperoni with anchovies and jalapeños as a pregnant peace offering. There, in the roped-off waiting area, I sipped draft beer with other men whose orders were baking. "I'm going to be a father soon," I'd confess to one man or another. The newness of this information startled us both. Once, a man thought I'd said that I had just *become* a father, and rounds were stood for all. That day, there seemed no better smell on earth than spicy sauces simmering and the odor of baking bread. The wait-ress gave me my pizza wrapped in white paper which reminded me of gifts wrapped for children on their birthdays. I held the cardboard circle by its circumference because the bottom was so hot. It rode up the mountain to our cottage in the front seat like an honored guest.

"Look at what I've brought." I got out crushed red peppers and garlic salt and Romano cheese as Lisa rubbed her eyes from an afternoon nap.

"Let's make that fight our last fight." Lisa was so hungry with the baby that she stuffed a whole piece into her mouth before she realized she was eating like a starved person. "You don't under-stand how it is to be hungry like this."

I told her to eat, please eat; there was all the pizza in the world for her hunger. I said we were a husband and a wife with a baby on the way, by God, so she shouldn't be embarrassed. Later in the night, when the lovemaking was over and I wandered around the house, I'd stand by the window and get lonely and hungry all over again. Then I'd remember the leftover pizza and stand eat-ing it in the staircase of light cast by the open refrigerator.

"Who is it? *What do you want?*" Lisa once asked when she had awoken and found me missing. Her face was scared, and she gripped a bookend to clobber a burglar. She held it hefted and poised for business. We both laughed at what she had found—no intruder, just her husband. I was down on my knees, not praying but thinking about that night when the noise of heavy labor started.

OPAL SLAMMED the screen door and called me, her hands bunched angrily on her hips. She grabbed my arm and shook her head "no" at the beer in my fist as I tried to rush inside to Lisa. Since the midwives had driven up in their Jeep—*hunters* drive cars like that, I had thought—the house had become something other than my own. I felt as if I should apologize for being there.

"This isn't a party," said Opal. "Ruby shouldn't drink—she's allergic to alcohol."

"This has gone far enough," I said. "I'm calling an ambulance and getting my wife to the hospital. And if the least thing is wrong with Lisa and the baby, I'll sue you for everything you own, down to your underwear."

"Calm down." Opal led me into my living room.

Lisa was hunched in a squatting position, hugging an arm of the couch. Two old fans in the windows behind her grudgingly created a breeze. Their motion made the evening sun's light swim on the floor like heat on a distant bend of road. Ruby stepped into this light to smooth back Lisa's hair. Lisa was naked and shuddering with sweat and her gravidness. She moaned from a place inside herself I had never heard from. If she called to me from that place, how would I travel to her? When Opal knelt to massage oil into Lisa's labia majora, I caught fire with jealousy.

"Let *me* do that." I lathered my hands with oil and began rubbing without looking at midwife Opal. The odd sensation of rubbing my wife's vagina in front of visitors struck me. I fought the strange urge to tickle Lisa's clitoris while these houseguests watched. I got an erection and stretched on the floor to hide it when something like a marbled egg peeked at me from Lisa's vagina.

"That's the baby's head," explained Opal. She promised the baby would work free of the amniotic sac before descending the birth canal. I remembered reading in a home birth book that a good "birth partner"—they never used the words "father" or "husband"—tried to show the laboring mother what was transpiring. After I ran to the bathroom to get my shaving mirror, I positioned it under Lisa. Opal stepped back and watched Lisa and me the way someone does when they catch something old in a new light. She worked more oil into her hands. She was a large woman who resembled a man when you caught her the wrong way. Her husband deserted her periodically, and it showed in her face, along with all the babies she had delivered. Her fingers were tiny, like those children in India who weave complicated tapestries. She explained to me that the birth was still some hours away, that Lisa wasn't even six centimeters dilated yet, that the labor was going nicely, and that things would proceed in the manner that nature ordained them. I repeated this midwife's words to Lisa—even "ordained"—exactly as she had said them, as if they were a litany, and neither woman rebuked me for the repetition. Strangely, I noticed my hands were shaking and the room had collapsed like a sheet blown off a clothesline. I kept thinking the phone was ringing and got up to answer it.

"Hello." The thing still rang though the receiver was clearly in my hand. "We're having a baby here, so could you call back later? Don't worry, everything is under control."

He's going to swoon, someone said, and I did.

RUBY GAVE me a pep talk as I sat outside on the steps with my head between my legs. She assured me that many men balked at the rigors of childbirth. Things would get messier—which was something I didn't want to hear. I felt guilty for being secretly glad the pain was Lisa's and not my own. Ruby had draped a wet towel over my head, so all I could see in the fading evening light were my feet and her hand when it brought smelling salts. I said I felt like a person in a movie theater afraid to look at the frightening scenes.

"You're disassociating yourself from her pain," claimed Ruby.

I told her I put little stock in psychology.

"Then what *do* you believe in?"

Her question unsettled me. More than once, Lisa had complained my lack of spiritual conviction was a serious character flaw. Our house on the top of the mountain gave way to miles of woods which she sometimes walked through, returning from the old logging road positively giddy with nature. What do you do when you're not the type of man whose soul quakes at sunsets? You believe in palpable things—the heft of her breasts in your hand or the good weariness you feel after turning a patch of stony soil into a garden. Once, before we were married, Lisa had tried to explain our love to me while she did her Tai Chi exercises naked. All I understood was the peaceful feeling of a lazy morning which would lead to a shower together, and back to bed. The light in the room was like that done by old masters, and I had fallen in love and wanted to make a baby; people had been chasing this type of happiness all the way back to Adam.

"I'm not sure what I believe in," I said to Ruby. "I've not been myself lately, with all this baby business. The fact is," and I was sad to admit this, "I believe in things you can feel and see. No offense."

"None taken."

"Sex. I suppose I believe in sex."

"Your belief in that is why we're here."

"I really can't name what I believe in."

Ruby turned to look at me with her good eye's narrow vision. "Now you're starting to understand. But still, you seem nervous." I remarked another beer would fix that. "No," she said.

"Neither of us is going to drink. What we have to do is find another way of calming your nerves. What do you do to relax?"

"I throw horseshoes." Two boxed pits sat up on the hill.

"Let's play," she said.

"It wouldn't be fair, Ruby. You're nearly blind. Besides, there's not enough light left to see things clearly."

"That'll even things up," said Ruby.

WHAT FOLLOWED was a lesson in humility. Ruby skunked me four games straight. First, she had me walk her the distance between the pits. At each stob she backed up and bumped her calf against the metal. She swung the shoes to test their weight and balance and clanked them together like tuning forks to listen to their ringing. She threw a sidewinder—something only the old-timers can master—and she threw all ringers. The moon hadn't risen yet, and what little light that fell from the stars was lost in the shadows of the woods near where we played. I complained there had to be a trick involved; how could someone connect with something they couldn't see? Then Ruby explained she had once toured county fairs with a carnival sideshow which specialized in wagering on oddities. Ruby and her partner made money challenging oncomers they could beat blindfolded. According to Ruby, she had once thrown nothing but blindfolded ringers for a solid month.

Consider this: a guy thinks he's good in horseshoes; hell, he's won some bucks at barbecues and even a county fair championship trophy. Then he finds himself at a carnival where someone is willing to play him blindfolded. He figures he can triple the fifty in his wallet. The poor sap doesn't understand he's whipped before he's even started. He's an honest fellow who believes he can control the game's outcome if he concentrates enough and wills it so. This belief was money in Ruby's pocket.

"Ruby." I felt a sudden need to confess. "Lisa and I argue a lot.

We smash dishes and say things which can't ever be taken back. Then we make love, and though I'm not sure if divorce isn't around the corner, I quit worrying. She has this way of looking into my eyes and leaning into me before she goes to sleep which makes everything worth it. She seems as big as a church when this happens, and all I know to do is wrap my arms around her and hold on."

"Shhh," said Ruby. "Shut your eyes and enjoy the calm before you throw."

I did. I shut my eyes—why not, they were useless in this game she had mastered. Of all the things to think of, I remembered the day Lisa had announced she was pregnant. We had gotten in the car and driven toward Oklahoma in the newly wintered landscape. I tried imagining the fields thick with oats and hay while Lisa listed the knickknacks the baby would need and tested the sound of names. *"Listen,"* Lisa had urged, pointing to her stomach. Of course it was too early to hear anything, but I had listened. Lisa had guided the steering wheel as I worked the gas and set my head in her lap. She remarked that driving like this was risky business; what wasn't, I said bullishly. I couldn't see where we were going and didn't care; I was a man with his ear cocked toward the oldest of feelings. Then I sat up and hammered the horn and flashed my lights at oncoming motorists, as if to warn them of some danger we had successfully navigated. I gave a little war whoop and yelled out the just-opened window that I was going to be a father. Lisa picked up the spirit and let loose with a "yahoo" of her own. Then we had stuck our arms out the window like kids, as if to grapple with and grab at something as airy as our passage, with everything around us quiet like church.

I pitched my horseshoe toward this feeling.

IF THERE is a lesson to be learned from witnessing birth, then it is that all things are urged urgently into being. Midwife Ruby had left me to my blind horseshoe throwing—an art I would never master. I felt as if I had to *do* something, so I chain-smoked cigarettes and gathered the herbs as she had instructed. Then I dug a hole in the garden for the placenta, deep, to keep away raccoons and harm. I felt like a man either searching for or burying hidden secrets. Every light in the house was ablaze, and now and then Lisa would pass by a window as she searched for the room where she would have our baby.

Opal came to the back porch and said, "Lisa's asking for you. The time is getting close."

"When will it happen?"

"Soon. Go inside now."

I wandered inside the strangeness of my own house. The room smelled of labor. Now and then Lisa struggled up and paced and grunted and pulled me close for a hug. It was like trying to encircle a planet. When she fell back onto the couch where she had decided to have the baby, she squeezed my shoulder until I saw her pain as white dots in my clenched eyes. Lisa loosened her grip, and Ruby wiped her with wet towels and cool washrags. Opal suggested I ready the herbal bath for Lisa and the baby. I put herbs named comfrey and uva-ursi and shepherd's purse and sea salt in a cheesecloth, which I boiled. Then I stoppered the tub and poured in potful after potful of the witch's brew. There was even garlic in this concoction. This was water which the midwives promised would heal.

"The baby's coming," said Opal. A hairy head tried to crown, then slid back in. Ruby was down there helping, too. Her eyes looked off to the side, and I wondered if I were crazy to allow a nearly blind midwife to touch Lisa. Then something gave inside me and I put my faith in this woman. Ruby was predicting the baby's position as that of a stargazer, which meant that it would come into the world with its eyes oriented toward the heavens. Stargazers are difficult babies to pass, warned Ruby; they require much pushing, and they strain the birth muscles. Opal checked the fetal heartbeat with a stethoscope while Ruby tested Lisa's abdomen with presses and movements of her fingertips. She was seeing with her hands. This fascinated me. Think of it—all the lives coaxed into being with fingers impartial to the misfortunes those lives would winter. These were hands that fluttered over their work like weavers of an old tapestry. They could envision heaven or hell on the ceiling of a chapel, and feel good about it. These were *midwives'* hands.

"Please push," I said to Lisa. I maneuvered myself between her legs and readied my hands to catch what was headed my way. Lisa's eyes rolled back into their sockets until nothing but the whites showed, as they did when we made love, and I understood she had taken off for a place inside herself that she alone could visit. I squatted there putting together what I knew. I had drunk some beer with a nearly blind midwife and swooned and gotten soundly thrashed in horseshoes. I would catch the baby and cut the umbilical cord. When the birth was over, I would bury the placenta in my garden, and some years later, when my child had angrily tossed away a kitten which fell to its death down a flight of stairs, I'd make my child hold death as I dug the hole, and I'd remember burying that placenta while through the bathroom window I watched the midwives lowering Lisa and then the baby into water as dark as things we forget. But I didn't know any of this that night I became a father. All I knew was that everything my child might become seemed somewhere outside, keeping a patient and respectable distance.

But what I cannot account for, even now, is the dizzying sensation that the room had taken off and gathered speed and somehow grown more spacious than the largest coliseum. Here was a place as exterior as interior that I would be allowed to visit only a few times in my life. This room was like traveling with Lisa when I had sounded the horn to announce our pregnancy to homeward-bound travelers, and they had dimmed then brightened their lights in acknowledgment of the hazards of safe passage. Suddenly the world and all the dangers my son Fisher would ride seemed a place which I could tame. No man can do that, though he must try, and I would have to learn to deliver us to whatever still places this holy knowledge afforded.

What It Cost Travelers

WHEN I was thirty-five and freshly separated and still a stouthearted pilgrim to myself, I took a job on the Gulf Coast swindling people. I sold fake trailer lot deeds to investors with souls more crooked than my own. This stint was my father-in-law's brainchild and his prescription for what I needed—a working vacation designed to clear myself of debt while I charted the direction of my life and tenuous marriage. Three divorces had taught him this tactic. My own marriage had floundered after a drunken night when my son's rocking horse sailed through the picture window. I had been convinced my wife, Lisa, had cuckolded me with the young Hispanic groundskeeper of the apartment complex she managed. I wish I could confess that my character was roomy enough to dismiss my suspicions or that I had proof of her infidelity, but I didn't. Instead, I got the guy deported as an illegal alien, and in recompense Lisa moved me to a vacant apartment and changed the locks on our door. She called a lawyer who ran No Contest Divorce ads on Houston TV. When I began canceling the night classes I taught to conduct surveillance on my own home and love, I felt like a changeling. My dreams filled with sirens—both police and nymph—so I made some excuses and headed south.

"Why are you sending back *arrowheads?*" Lisa asked the first time I called. "Most fathers would mail stuffed animals or fairy tale books." The fake lots sat on an old Indian burial ground, and after rooking clients, I poked with a mattock for relics. The souvenir flint pieces seemed a roundabout way of explaining what I was searching for. I posted packages of small ones designed to down birds and deer and larger ones fashioned for humans.

"I'm not most fathers," I said.

"You got that right. That window cost two-hundred-fifty to replace."

"They're nice arrowheads," I said. "Besides, I thought maybe we could mount them on gold chains and market them as necklaces."

"Damn you, have you gone into cahoots with Daddy again?" Lisa believed I was fishing and airing my soul for the required separation period. Also, her father and I had once summoned some quick money by creatively adjusting insurance claims.

"No, honey," I lied.

"I have a *suitor* at the door." Vivaldi's *Four Seasons*—the tape we listened to before making love—was playing. "Don't call back tonight." She hung up and unhooked the phone.

After that, I only called when I was desperate to hear her voice quicken my pulse. She didn't want me back—of that she was sure. Sometimes she put our son on the phone to illustrate the new sounds learned in my absence, and his babbling reminded me of happier times when I owned the best love had to offer.

"Who is this Rob Roberts guy?" Lisa asked after one of those conversations. "Why is he calling *here* for you all the time?" I feared I had swindled him until I remembered I'd had a car accident with him on the way down, outside Houston. He could have been my double, except for his red hair and Vandyke. During heavy rains, his car had planed, and my Winnebago with the eighteen-foot Wellcraft boat in tow left his car totaled. The Winnebago lost a headlight, but we were both unscratched. The police decided no fault, and Rob Roberts and I exchanged insurance cards. He asked for a ride to Angleton, the nearest town. I told Lisa that Rob Roberts quickly located the Winnebago's bar and helped himself to my Old Crow. Then he produced a wallet and showed pictures of his children from different marriages. I suspected the kids weren't even his, that they came with the wallet like those pictures in the frames at K-Mart. Lisa and I called these people laminites, and I was smart enough not to tell her his wallet was filled with people he didn't know.

"I guess I gave the guy our home number without thinking," I said.

"Don't get any ideas about coming back before the thirty days are over," she said. "And by the way, I'm sure that whatever it is you're doing down there, it's illegal. Do you want your son to visit you behind bars?"

The investors I fleeced were savings and loan officers who would write off the loss rather than risk prosecution and the embarrassment of an audit. Their hands were slick with ill-gotten oil rights and other people's money. The real estate was called Paráiso, and some days I sold as many as twenty parcels of paradise to people convinced they were stealing from me. The land was a short half-mile off Galveston Bay—in La Porte—and after a week I didn't notice the stink of the dioxins or the sulfuric smell from the chemical plants and many refineries. The breeze from the bay kept what I called the furies (botflies and mosquitoes) farther inland, and in the mornings—which is the time for sweetheart deals—the salty air was laced with diesel odors as tugboats ferried tankers into port or back to the gulf. After selling unreal real estate, I'd jig with mud minnows for flounder off sandbars which the tide would sink.

Certain afternoons, I drank at Marybelle's, where astronauts once celebrated before getting shot into outer space. The owner of the bar could remember Neil Armstrong drunk and pointing heavenward as he bellowed that, by God, he would travel to the moon and bring back a piece of it. The story went that John Wayne, on a lost weekend, held the record at Marybelle's for the most crabs eaten at a single sitting. Outlined holes in the ceiling tiles proved he had fired his six-shooter raucously in Texas fashion, before the Hollywood helicopter whisked him away to make the movie about the grit it took to tame America. By the time I drank there, in the early 1990s, the clientele were mainly just-paid oil riggers and shrimpers and wealthy widows who preferred rough, impermanent men. I drank beer bumped with schnapps while people formed couples, feeling guilty my love was not Hollywood material. I was a man with a failed marriage, sitting in a bar lined with signed pictures of men who had ridden into sunsets and left footprints on the moon. Behind me, newly formed couples laughed as they understood they would spend a quick night together. That sound and the smell of Creole-seasoned crabs and the first evening stars on the water made me feel like a missing person.

This French leave feeling prompted me to buy some beer and shrimp and drive to Sandy's house. She worked as my secretary to add a legitimate quality to my dealings. She claimed she didn't mind my job required that I deceived people as I quickly passed through. Her two grade-school kids—little Glen and Glenda—still attended the special school in Johnson City built to accommodate the children of astronaut trainees and engineers who worked at the Space Center. Her husband, Big Glen, had been an engineer who helped with the tile work on *Challenger* before suffering a nervous breakdown. He now thought Sandy was his sister and his children were orphans she had kindly adopted. We all sat at the table layered with newspapers and tossed the shrimp shells in a central heap like any normal family. We passed garlic butter and cocktail sauce while the kids crawled all over me and searched my pockets for the Hershey's Kisses I brought as booty. Big Glen even deferred the largest shrimp to me, as if *he* were a moocher in *my* house. He slept in a little pop-up camper in the backyard, working late into the night on balsa wood airplanes constructed meticulously to scale. Sandy and I were careful to keep the bedroom door locked when we made love. The situation was indecent, but I wasn't her first lover since Glen's breakdown, and I had misplaced the scrupulous part of myself which could care. The Gulf Coast was like that—full of people whose luck had tricked them into risking anything in order to rediscover what they had lost.

I MARRIED up in life, and Lisa would have disapproved of Sandy. She lived in a cul-de-sac in a frame house nearly identical to the other one hundred in a development no one had bothered to name. A few hopelessly wind-crooked pines or a spindly poplar ornamented the more industrious renters' yards, along with ceramic flamingoes and birdbaths and a rock garden or two. Each house had a carport and a slab concrete patio. A few yards boasted above-ground swimming pools because the bay there was unfit for swimming. The poor soil yielded few vegetable gardens—just crabgrass and sandburs. This was one step up from a trailer park. The women had jobs and the men were often bandaged or in casts as they bent over the hood of a car, inspecting its guts.

Certain mornings, the whole place made me melancholy for my childhood and the life I had outdistanced. I'd say the hell with swindling people and piddle around the house sipping coffee laced with Old Crow as I sat by a window investigating these people's lives. Dressed in Sandy's checkered robe and her furry bunny slippers, I felt like a man on vacation who had abandoned the rules of home. These were people like those from my child-hood, and they brought forth rummaged memories. Once, just after dawn, I witnessed one neighbor scooping a shovel full of dog shit from his yard. He plopped it on the dog owner's car hood. Then he pulled out Old Jake and shot a fine stream on the fender and back tire. His wife admired him from the patio door, urging him to hurry and to arc it higher. Another time, a man pulled a woman from a car and stripped off her shirt. He lay back on the trunk and begged her to squirt milk in his face. She was still plump with maternity's weight, and she screamed she wanted more money. My only conversation with one of Sandy's neigh-bors involved dimes. I had gone to the Winnebago for more bourbon. A portly man hurried over as I crossed the yard. He claimed to have quit drinking for a month, until that morning, when he had found the dimes. He held out a coffee cup and asked for straight whiskey. He said his first or second wife—he couldn't remember—wore bunny slippers like mine. When he asked to try one on, I obliged. Neither of us thought the moment odd.

"I must have done this, but I don't remember." He showed me a cigar box full of dimes, grouped in hundreds in sandwich bag-gies. "See here, there's my name on the box."

He said he'd decided to quit the booze and tidy up his life, and he found—of all things—plastic baggies full of dimes stashed at the back of his closet, where he kept girlie magazines and mate-less socks. These were simply dimes—not collector's items—and he had two cigar boxes full of these things he had no reason to save. *Why dimes,* he kept asking. He was afraid to look in his freezer—hell, it might be stacked with dead cats! He confessed he had never collected anything but wives and trouble and once, as a kid, some wishbones. He asked me what type of desperate person would sit up late nights drinking and putting dimes in plastic bags? When I gave him another drink, he tried to pay for it with a baggie of horded silver.

I shut Sandy's curtain and tried to imagine these people in happy moments—grilling fat porterhouses over a perfectly laid fire, or as honored guests at a wedding party where everyone smiled awkwardly in rented formal attire while the photographer snapped a group picture. What I wondered most was why good fortune was rented too. This thought sent me wandering through Sandy's house. The urge to protect my surrogate family and the real one I had left behind was as startling as any quickening. I peeped in on sleeping Sandy, then checked on little Glen and Glenda, tucking the sheets around their chin if the air was too cool or easing back the bedcovers if sweat had beaded on their foreheads. Once, I caught myself kissing those two kids on their cheeks, as I had done to my own son. Of all the things to think about, I remembered a day in Arkansas when Lisa and I were newlyweds. We were snowed-in and happy. On a bet, I had run outside naked and made a snow angel in the nearest drift. Lisa stood by the living room window with her hands on her hips as she shook her head approvingly at my tomfoolery. My flannel shirt she wore had fallen open, exposing her breasts and the half-moon marks her bikini top had hidden from the summer sun. She looked my way thoughtfully, studying her reflection and my nakedness against the winter landscape. I thought: I am somehow contained in her image. Back inside, she warmed me up with lazy winter love in a chair by the gas heater. Sex always made her sleepy, while it fueled me. She slept, and I dressed and went outside and held my cupped face to every window. The slipcover of the chair still held our rough imprint, and the scented candles Lisa lit for such occasions reminded me of hopeful birthdays. At each window I breathed on a pane and wiped through my breath like a kid in front of a department store display. A neighbor walking by to check his mail at the bottom of the mountain hailed me. Did he think I was checking for cracked panes or air leaks, or had he ever walked outside his own happiness and cased it like a burglar? I had stood there, a traveler to myself, wanting only to safekeep this good feeling and to delay its passage. This was how I felt watching Sandy's kids sleep. What would I have said if either child had awoken and asked what I was doing there in their mother's robe and slippers? That I was a man on the mend passing through their lives? A more honest response would have included the fact that I was caught up in a motion which was no one's to own.

SATURDAYS, MY father-in-law rendezvoused with me at Marybelle's to counsel me on thievery and love. Sandy gave him his share of the money wrapped as a gift with festive paper and a bright bow. He insisted she be present at these exchanges.

"That way, you'll be less likely to rat on us. Conspiracy to commit fraud is a crime too, and what we have here is a conspiracy."

Each week he gave me a list of investors he had scouted and a new fake ID. I was Yancey McCalister, Bucky Earl Mays III, Thurgood Owens, and Parker T. Wiley. He selected the names from the *Houston Chronicle*'s obituary section and credit-checked them to insure that the investors would be pleased with net worth and solvency. Their wills had yet to be probated; these were souls so newly dead they still received mail. Using these assumed names, I baited greedy loan officers with a forged dual contract for deed and asked them for 10 percent of the property's value. Then I allowed them to haggle me down to 5 percent so that they could sense desperation in my situation. "Let them smell foreclosure," my father-in-law always said. "Sign a default clause promising the land is theirs if you don't pay back the loan in a month."

Sandy's job was to shuffle the paperwork and flirt and mix the drinks as she and I drove the bankers to appraise the property. I'd hint of a possible divorce—a lie must be seasoned with a little truth—and they sympathized. I posed as a man selling what he could before misfortune visited, and they offered me no more than 5 percent for my misery. The month I toured the Gulf Coast, I swindled two loan officers a week, but I could have easily fleeced more. Of the eight, seven used appraisers they had bribed, and all of them asked point-blank if a quick roll with Sandy were part of the deal. One banker bragged that, before the advent of his second divorce, he'd sold his custom bass boat for fifty cents to an old man who sold minnows at a bait shop he frequented—just so his wife would be furious. "Two quarters," he'd said to her. "Enough to cover your eyes when you're dead." He claimed the old man's dream was to die happily in that boat, a big bass running while the drag screamed like a blender. The banker confided it was the one good thing he'd done in his life except adopting ten starving children advertised on TV. "And I did it for vendetta," he said. This was the only time I felt remorse as I signed a certified check.

"Don't go moral on me," my father-in-law said when I recounted the story. "Fleece two a week—no more—and we won't get caught. We're a little part of something bigger than Texas." He was right; we were a small part of what would be named the savings and loan scandal.

"Look at the seal on that baby," my father-in-law said that second Saturday at Marybelle's. "That's impressive work, isn't it?" He handed me a forged contract for deed and my weekly identity. Paperclipped to the edge of the document was a snapshot of Lisa and me on our honeymoon, sunburnt and happy and hoisting a forty-pound king mackerel.

"What's this supposed to mean?"

"Richard." The use of my real name jolted me. "She's throwing things like this out. I'm sorry. It's not a good sign. When I told Lisa we were going speckled-trout fishing this weekend, she asked me to get you to sign these." He handed me a preliminary copy of the divorce and a waiver of my right to contest. The child support and visitation rights were generous, but when I signed the documents I fought the crazy urge to use a name resurrected from the dead. Then he gave me a letter from my insurance company stating Rob Roberts was claiming back injuries from the car accident. Wasn't I hurt too? Allstate queried. If so, we could countersue. The business card of a chiropractor not mentioned in the letter was inside the envelope. Sandy read the letter with interest.

"You can't sue him," she said.

"She's right." My father-in-law tore up the letter and card. "That's how people get caught. One scam at a time." He winked at Sandy. "Right?"

"But the guy wasn't hurt. He's a goddamned crook. He's swindling people." The anger in my voice surprised me. Sandy and my father-in-law laughed; what did I think *we* were doing? By evening, when Venus and the first stars were mirrored in the heavens and on the water like a string of cheap lights, we had only to repeat *he's a swindler* and we'd laugh until we lost our breath. After my father-in-law left, Sandy and I lingered to watch sailboats motor toward the pass leading to the gulf. Flashing beacons warned of pilings which each year claimed the lives of wreckless boaters. Above us a rainbow-shaped bridge carried the highway toward Houston and old feelings and broken vows. For a quick second or two, I tortured myself with an image of Lisa, legs hoisted in the crooks of some stranger's arms as she demanded him to love deeper, harder.

"Men like you like them beautiful, don't they Richard?" Sandy had removed the photograph of Lisa and me from my shirt pocket. She stood there, one woman appraising the image of another. The swiftness of my reflex to stop her when she pretended to shred the picture startled me.

"I won't tear up your honeymoon picture of things." She stuffed the snapshot back in my pocket. "I can't be her—hell, I don't want to be. I like my men rumpled and on the lam. Like you." We kissed under a moon imprinted with a wanderer's urge. She laughed, bit my lips, pulled away. "The guy before you once bet me in a poker game as part of the pot. I didn't get mad, Richard. I *liked* it. Part of me wanted his full house to lose, so I could watch his face as I left with the winner."

"And if his full house had gotten beat?" I asked. "What then?"

"I would have gone back to him the next day and shown him what he had wagered and lost. I would have screwed him silly. Which is what I'm going to do to you tonight."

We took the back roads to a stretch of the gulf between Freeport and San Luis Pass, past broken and twisted windmills known locally as President Carter's Folly. High winds had thwarted the utopian idea that electricity could be produced cleanly here. Sandy drove the Winnebago while I mixed drinks and adjusted the radio to pleasant stations. We found an access road and drove up the beach. The way was lined with groups of cars parked side-by-side like drive-in moviegoers. Tires, lumber, and stumps of great trees washed down from the Trinity River or another tributary burned in bonfires around which people— mostly teenagers and migrant workers who couldn't afford a motel room—gathered. Here and there lonely men angled for big skate and gafftop and cast purse nets for bait fish. At night the gulf seemed a substantial paradise; the oil balls and garbage were hidden. Naked lovers proud of their sport raced through our headlights to the surf. When Sandy asked had I ever made love in the gulf, I was ashamed to admit I hadn't. We parked the Win-nebago along a deserted stretch.

"Leave your clothes on," she said. "We'll undress each other in the water."

We waded past the breakers, to our chests. Schools of skittish mullet splashed and jumped. "Throw it all away," Sandy whispered as we embraced. She helped me with my shirt, whirled it around her head like a lasso, and let it fly. I stepped out of my pants and boxers as soon as she ripped them down. My lips and hands tested the difference between this woman's geography and the image of the one drifting away with my shirt. For an instant I panicked; the wallet floating away contained no money but my one true ID. Then Sandy guided me inside her, and I didn't care. Midway through love she pulled my face from her breasts and held it breath-close to hers.

"We could run away together and start fresh somewhere out west where we have no history." She licked and bit my nipples.

"What about your kids?"

"We'd take them, of course."

"And Glen?"

Sandy's mouth tugged my earlobe. "Glen doesn't know who he is. We could stick him in an institution. Or we could carry him with us, if you feel that guilty."

"So I'm your ticket out of here?"

"Wasn't Lisa *your* passport? Didn't *you* marry up?" Then she moved hard against me and whispered, "Lisa has felt this with other people." The mention of Lisa coupled made me come.

"Good?" Sandy guided my hand to our joining, which felt borderless.

"Oh, Richard," she said. "Why do people get so possessive about this feeling? Love is lent. Hell, it's usury."

A WEEK after my wallet drifted away, the Coast Guard—not an FBI investigator—nearly arrested me for fraud. By midweek I

had swindled my quota and decided to go offshore fishing. Sandy
insisted I take Glen; he had once loved to fish, and the time alone
with the kids would allow her to explain the trip out west to
which I had halfheartedly conceded.

"We'll fly to Reno, gamble some, and scout out the prospects
there." She said Glen would watch the kids until we returned for
them. We would do a few quick land deals, then live an honest
life in Wyoming or Montana, where property was reasonable
and there was space enough to start over. "Just like pioneers," she
claimed. The kids would frolic on horseback through streams,
and summers my son would visit and stouten himself on the
trout we would catch. All this happiness could be ours if we simply traveled there. Sandy was beside me in the Wellcraft helping
stow away enough gear for two nights on the water as she said
this.

"Too much of my life has been like this trailered boat,
Richard. All packed and ready to go with no place to put in. You
do believe we can make a go of it?"

"Yes."

"You wouldn't con me, would you?" Her laugh rasped as she
walked her fingers up my chest and poked my nose. "You'll learn
to love me." Though she didn't say *state's evidence,* we both
thought it.

"You can't con an honest person," I said.

"You remember that."

"We can't forget *these.* " Glen trotted from the house with car-
tridges for his .22-caliber pistol. He liked to shoot sharks at night.

"It would be terrible if someone got hurt with that gun,"
Sandy said.

"What's that supposed to mean?" I asked.

"It means careless people get hurt on boats all the time. Don't
you be one of them."

As we left, Sandy and the kids formed a little group on the

patio and called our names. The kids still called Glen Dad, but he was none the wiser for it.

"I don't know why they call me that," he said as we drove away from the cul-de-sac. "But I like it." Sandy had claimed that being with Glen was like living with a ghost. He had gone to a place where he couldn't be reached, she'd said.

Which was exactly how I felt about my own life and marriage as we launched at dusk from Texas City. Along the way Vietnamese families washed their shrimp boats and picked crabs and conversed in their twangy language. The restaurants along the wharf were lit with festive lanterns under which couples sat with heads bent together. On the jetties, teenaged boys with their dates fished for whatever would bite. Glen mixed us drinks and sat beside me at the console pointing at the beacons and absently naming the first constellations. Another big drink convinced me we all had selective amnesia, and I joined in his naming of the heavens. He scrunched his brow and remembered from somewhere that men on boats drinking whiskey liked to sing.

"What do you like to sing?" I asked.

"Hymns." He was as chock-full of them as a Methodist hymnal, and I joined in where I could. He had been a baritone in a barbershop quartet, so mainly I drank whiskey and listened. We were far enough out that land had fallen from sight, and our wake turned phosphorescent as night spilled from the crown of the sky. Glen's hymns reminded me of my father's stories that the New World had been an Eden before the Europeans ruined it. My father said the entire East Coast had been covered with vines whose roots were a single Eve of a wild grape plant. My father got excited when he imagined that plant and the settlers who saw it that first morning the ship made landfall. They knew they had arrived somewhere—but where? So much of this New World was uncharted. They didn't even know if the inhabitants would shower them with gifts or arrows. Most of those settlers were escaping debts back home or seeking their fortunes. All of them saw in the tangled landscape whatever happiness their hands could carve. They were at that point in their lives where terra incognita—that's how it was listed on the old maps—became the life they would own. Amidst the good cheer of bottles uncorked to toast their arrival, they would wonder if something were beginning or ending. Sitting beside Glen as he sang hymns, I wondered: Had they truly discovered a New World, or had they simply wandered closer to the source of their troubles?

WE TIED up to a working oil rig with floodlights and a warning horn which sounded at lugubrious intervals. I fished for small bonita which I sliced into ribbons and tossed overboard for chum. Soon enough, the sharks came in shadowy droves, and the larger ones made a mess of the tackle, but the sixty pounders were ours for the taking. Glen peppered them with his .22 when I got them alongside the boat.

"I got your number, you bastard." He jerked the trigger so rapidly the shots sounded like a string of firecrackers. He emptied whole clips into them. How could he remember hymns or how to shoot sharks, but not the feel of his wife? He had a loaded gun, and now was not a good time for his memory to return.

Two bored oil riggers came down the catwalk to investigate the noise. I apologized if our sport disturbed their sleep. "Should we find an uninhabited rig?" I asked.

"The day's the same as the night out here," the one with thick glasses said. He explained they slept in windowless rooms so dark they needed flashlights to find the light switch. "We're just two geologists getting in some offshore time. The company requires it. The rig runs itself." Then he asked if they could join in the fun; his buddy had snuck a .38 aboard the platform.

"Back in a minute!" the owner yelled. The one with glasses asked could he run a shark on our tackle.

"I've never caught a fish before." He cleaned his glasses on his shirt as he confessed. "I got a stuffed sailfish on my wall, big sucker, five feet—even my wife thinks I caught it." When he lay down on the catwalk, I handed up a big Penn reel on a broomstick-thick rod, baited and ready to go. He fumbled puzzledly with the equipment. "Don't tell my buddy—he thinks I caught that fish."

"I won't. Hell, I'll never see you again." I winked and he followed my instructions expertly. By the time his co-worker returned, the rod was bowed mightily with a big hammerhead. They called the fish "Jaws" and passed the rod back and forth so that each could share this pull-you-down feeling.

"I told you fishing was a spiritual thing," the guy with the store-bought sailfish said to his buddy. When the big shark's white underside thrashed on the surface, we cheered as Glen filled it with holes. The guy with the .38 fired like a carnivalgoer at a shooting gallery.

"Offshore time!" I couldn't tell if he were praising or cursing his fate. I had read somewhere that the fear of sharks is nearly universal, and looking into those obsidian eyes, I didn't doubt it. A shark could chop you in half and not care. It could blindside your dear grandmother as she floated past the breakers and called for the family to come join her—the water was perfect for a swim. Here was something primordial, before evil itself, colder than the ice at the center of the world. You could lose yourself in a shark's eyes.

WHAT BROUGHT me back from the realm of the dead was what it cost travelers. At sunrise we unhitched from the rig after the geologist explained our position on his topographical maps. The sailfish guy asked sheepishly if he could buy my rod and reel; he'd left *his* gear on the mainland, and they had three more days to kill here at the edge of the world. They had strung two big sharks

from the catwalk like huge crows on fence posts, and they had
tired of taking pictures.

"Keep the rod," I said. "What good is money out here?" Besides, the rod and reel belonged to my father-in-law. When he
produced his wallet, I repeated I didn't want any money.

"Go get some of the canned goods we got upstairs," he com-
manded his buddy. Then he handed me a picture of himself with
a woman and kid, bunched in a department store photo booth,
clowning at the camera. "That's who I am," he said. "That's my
family."

When I started to reciprocate, I remembered my lost wallet.
"I don't have anything like that to give you."

He misunderstood. "I'm glad *I* have a family." He said he didn't
see them enough, but he would soon. A promotion, and he'd
move back with them at home base, in Dallas, where they were
living. His co-worker lowered down a garbage bag full of canned
pâté and Danish hams and fancy crackers.

"Everything's in cans here—it lasts longer," my friend with the
fake sailfish said. "When I get back, I'm not eating anything in
cans for a goddamned month."

"Luck!" everyone yelled as we cast off. The less talkative geologist was an opera buff who had brought tapes and a jam box,
and we got under way to the preternatural sound of some Italian tenor broadcasting tragedy across the waters. At twenty miles
out, the gulf was a sparse forest of oil platforms, some inhabited,
some not. Glen drove, and I set out two rods with Rapalas as big
as the catfish of my childhood.

"Pick a rig and make a slow loop around it." I poured a bourbon and Coke and settled back to wait for the reels to sing.
When I dozed, Lisa appeared, in the bathtub, shaving her legs
with one hand in long, lazy strokes, while her other arm cradled
our nursing son. I was trying to get into that tub and make zany
faces at my dreaming self when Glen awoke me, holding a bro-

ken key in my face. The motor had stalled, and he had tried to start the boat with the lever in forward.

When I let loose with a string of invectives, he cowered like a kid and sulked with his back hunched away from me. To worsen our predicament, the Wellcraft had floated into an acre of sargasso. I got under the console to hot wire the engine, and I heard him splashing.

"What are you *doing?* Get back in the goddamned boat. This isn't the time for swimming." He whumped against the engine, and when I raised my head from under the console to see where he was, the wires connected and the engine fired. Glen was untangling the gulfweed from the motor—he'd climbed back into the boat and was leaning over the transom—and the propeller sheared his hand.

"Would you look at that," Glen said as I hurried to him. In shock, he inspected the stump bemusedly. As I fashioned a tourniquet, I remembered the Latin for left hand—*manus sinistra.* We were slammed against the stern, watching it tumble from memory and sight. That hand had held Sandy tightly, and it had formulated the precise mathematics required to shoot men into space and snatch them back safely. Was it waving hello or farewell or pointing a finger in accusation? Though unattached, that hand seemed to be grasping at things unseen.

Glen began vomiting and shaking, so I covered him with my poncho and screamed "Mayday" over the radio. When a crackly voice answered, I gave our position from the Loran. As I iced Glen's arm in the fish cooler, I thought of phantom limbs which itched and ached and must be soothed, though they beckoned from a part of yourself which no longer existed.

THE COAST Guard cruiser which answered our Mayday took us back to Texas City, where an ambulance waited. The dispatcher had called Sandy, who was en route. I was asked to stay behind to answer the questions the report required. When the Coast Guard seaman asked for some identification, I said I might have lost it during the confusion of the accident.

Just then Sandy rocketed into the parking lot, left the driver's door open, and hurried toward me. "Oh, Richard, when they called and said there'd been an accident, I thought it was *you*. The dispatcher didn't know the name of the injured person."

"Hold on here," said the seaman. "How come she calls you Richard, but the boat's registration number is listed in Jack McQueen's name?"

"He's my father-in-law. He lent me the boat to do a little fishing."

"But you signed Parker T. Wiley on the report. What's going on here?"

"Wait." Sandy went to the car and rifled through her glove compartment, then came back. "Here's his ID," said Sandy. "He left it in my car. You know how men misplace things."

"I still have to check." The seaman trotted off to his boat to call.

"Shut up. Let me do the talking." Then she commanded me to kiss her and squeeze her breasts and not stop. We were still like that when the seaman returned.

"Excuse me," the seaman said. "Okay. This Jack McQueen vouches for you, and your ID checks out clean as a whistle, but the name you signed is listed as dead. Now why would you want to use a dead man's name?"

"He just made up the name," said Sandy. "It's the name we always use when we check into hotels. You see he's down here fucking me and he doesn't want his wife or her lawyers to know." She stared at him. "Haven't *you* ever told someone you were who you weren't?"

This softened him. "While I was back at the boat, the hospital called and said your fishing buddy will be all right. He confirms it was an accident, but he's a little disoriented."

"He's not quite right," I said. "He sometimes forgets who he is."

"Seems to me like you got that problem too," said the seaman. "Now if you'll just scratch through that dead man's name and put your own, I'll file the report."

"How in the hell did you get my real ID?" I asked Sandy once we were driving to the hospital.

"I make duplicates of everything, in case something like this happens."

GLEN WAS released from the hospital five days later, and we hired a domestic to watch over his recovery. A relative would take care of the kids while Sandy and I went west. The plane tickets were bought and rooms were booked when, on the afternoon of the night I was to board a plane with Sandy, I had a change of heart. Or rather, I met a part of myself I had run into on the way down. I was drinking at Marybelle's while Sandy did some last-minute shopping, when Rob Roberts walked in wearing a neck brace and settled on the bar stool beside me.

"Remember me? We had ourselves a little accident outside Houston." He brushed back his thinning red hair and ordered a round.

"You're suing me, right?"

"Not you. Your insurance company." When he asked had my divorce come through, I told him that today was the day the required separation period was over. When I remembered those laminites in his wallet, I felt embarrassed for him. He kept adjusting his neck brace like an uncomfortable tie.

"I'll level with you, I'm not really hurt. The chiropractor and my lawyer make me wear this to court. When I saw your Winnebago in the parking lot, I slipped the brace on. You mind if I take the damned thing off?" When I said I didn't, he unbuckled it and placed it out of sight by his feet. He winked. "The women, they think you've got love problems when you wear this thing." When he asked if I were doing business down here or what, I answered I was taking a little vacation from myself.

Three drinks later, he said he would let me in on a little secret. His old girlfriend was in on a good scam. He couldn't quite figure out the whole deal, but his share in it was mildly lucrative.

"She's hooked up with this guy—she won't tell me who he is—but they do something with these fake IDs." He showed me an old one I had used with his picture on it. His ex-girlfriend— Sandy was her name—had once worked for the highway department and knew all about such things. "I think she's fallen for the sap. Says he's her ticket out of here. Anyway, do you realize all the things a guy can do with an ID like this?"

"I've got to be going," I said.

"No hard feeling about the insurance thing?"

"None. It's just insurance money."

"You're a *decent guy.*" When he said those two words, I knew what I would do. I left Marybelle's, where men had gone before they walked in space. Then I stopped by Western Union and wired money to Reno in Glen's name. I collected Glen and the kids and took them to the airport, where I had promised to meet Sandy. I got them first-class tickets and left before Sandy arrived.

Driving away, I envisioned the surprised look Sandy's face would register when the stewardess directed her to the aisle where Glen and the kids were waiting. When Glen handed her my note which told of the money wired and waiting in Reno, she'd weigh that against my deception and strap on the seatbelt. Once airborne, she'd order the drinks it took to gain perspective. She had her family sitting beside her, and most everything in the landscape she was leaving behind was rented. Arrangements could be made for a neighbor to send the necessities. Besides, the hotel was booked for two weeks, and I *had* delivered more than she expected—thirty-five thousand dollars—all of my gains. Around the Continental Divide, perhaps she'd start explaining to Glen who he was and what they had shared. This was wishful thinking, but I hoped the next morning in Nevada they'd all eat cold pizza—the kids' favorite breakfast—while chuckling at funny lines from old comedies as they plotted ways to invest their grubstake in happiness. What would keep Sandy from abandoning them? Would it be the thirty-five thousand that only Glen could collect, maternal instinct, or the way she searched her face in the hotel mirror the next morning and realized she had arrived where there were no easy answers. I never heard from Sandy again, and all I know of the Gulf Coast, I have confessed. Rob Roberts settled out of court for a meager two thousand. In my account of things—I was imagining now—Sandy tripled their money at Reno, and the God of travelers resurrected Glen's memory and their love, and they lived happily ever after. Only a swindler of dreams would allot them less, and I wasn't that. I was a man, headed home, wondering why his heart never fit inside its wanting.

Past Angleton, the road widened into four lanes with silhouettes of farmhouses. I eased upward through Texas into the uncharted feel of whatever lay just past the headlights. I thought of North Carolina—where I hailed from—and the grief my people's appetites brought them. My ancestors who were indentured paid for their passage with a portion of their lives. Imagine it— all the people who risked ocean crossings because they believed in a place where they could reinvent themselves. I kept envisioning my son's squeals of recognition when he saw me, and my hands and lips testing Lisa's familiar geography.

Then Houston appeared on the horizon like a city of lights. I pulled over to get a beer from the Wellcraft's cooler, and I sat at the boat's console drinking. There was no moon that night, or clouds, and I had an unobstructed view of the same heavens the old-timers had used for navigation. Another beer convinced me there was no difference between their situation and mine; no amount of traveling can save us from ourselves. We simply people new places with old sorrows and hopes. I began to see myself for who I was—a man struggling upward through a Leviathan dream called America. This thought drove me from the boat into a field of knee-deep roadside clover. I don't know why, but I started dancing. I even pulled out Old Jake, whooped up at the stars, and peed my initials like a kid. I began to formulate what the Gulf Coast would mean. It would be a place where I had swindled people and lost Lisa and any arrogant identification I would ever have with innocence. Why is it that, once you understand a place in the landscape of yourself, you've already left it behind?

Back on the road to Houston, I imagined my homecoming. For all I knew, some stranger could have settled into the apartment, and if this were the case, I would not start a scene. But suppose Lisa—not some sleepy-eyed lover—answered the door. Let's even say she left the porch light burning on the off chance that tonight was the night I'd wander back home. I'd ease up in low gear and strangle the urge to honk and disturb the nosy neighbors. I'd have another sack of arrowheads with me—not Cupid's flowers—and that would take some explaining. Rather than ring the bell, I'd knock to hold the full weight of my love in my hand. Maybe she'd be sewing as she did late nights, and she'd look through the peephole and recognize, through no fault of our own, we'd lost sight of the life we'd embarked upon. Locks would tumble as she opened the door.

"It's you," she'd say—something I couldn't deny. Then she'd invite me in to sleep on the couch, because our love had wandered and returned home more of a beggar than a prince. I'd do the wink trick with my eyes that was our secret, and when she returned the gesture, I'd be grateful but confused and filled with a sensation that even returning heroes could not deposit. This moment we were up against would be as real as bagged dimes and fake sailfish and the rest of our lives. Somehow, we would have to learn to inhabit this new space our love and its dissolution had created, where counterfeit promises were not acceptable payment for safe passage. We'd stand there under that left-on porch light, unsure, two people struggling to unknot what pilgrims called grace from their tangled hearts. This flat-footed moment is what it costs travelers. Before stepping over the threshold, I'd take Lisa's hand—not in marriage this time—and place it over my sternum, so she might at least understand the human racket my chest was making.

"Honey," I said that night. Somehow my voice had lost its ability to con. "Please, feel this."

When Love Gets Worn

I AM no stranger to love's errands—*this* is what I am thinking on Monday as I check my breath with a cupped hand before knocking on the door to what was once my own apartment. The mouthwash is cloaking my breakfast of Lone Stars and anchovies. The living-room window I once broke rattles, as Lisa and our son Fisher romp to the hokey-pokey tape. I wait before knocking, less to avoid interrupting their moment than to give myself time. For some months now, Lisa has been petitioning for an uncontested divorce, so once I'm inside, there will be final papers I don't want to read and sign. I stand there admiring the green paint and the MANAGER sign I lettered on her door. Lisa's father owns these one hundred apartments; Lisa manages them; and since I've returned from a bit of sordid business on the Gulf Coast, I've fattened my adjunct lecturer's wages by painting over the heel marks left by previous tenants. Threadbare money and frayed expectations and a tattered lifestyle got us here in Texas. where we unraveled. These are the types of apartments people rent when they are between more important pieces of their lives.

I am about to rifle through the garbage bag to see how my wife and son have been living, when Lisa opens the door.

"Checking up?" she asks.

"No," I say in my best I'm-not-checking-up-on-you voice. Once, shortly after she had boxed my belongings and instructed the groundskeeper to lug them to a vacant one-bedroom, she had caught me elbow-deep in her garbage, searching for evidence that another man had supplanted me. The moment, like the one we're having now, embarrassed us both.

"You never wore that suit very well," she says, shaking her head. "Come on in." I'm dressed absurdly in the clothes we wore when we married—down to my lucky boxer shorts with the trout on them—because I decided I should resemble either a funeralgoer or a wedding guest: The dark suit is somber enough for either occasion. I enter the familiar living room. My two-year-old son runs over to hug my legs and says, "Daddy, dance! Daddy, dance!" Lisa hands me the divorce settlement, and I ask her to rewind the tape. I make my face a mask of concentration as I pretend to read and dance with my son. The hokey-pokey requires you to put certain body parts in and out of an imaginary circle on the floor, and Fisher and I do that. I truly feel dismembered when I ask for a pen and sign the settlement. Lisa places the papers on the desk beside new leases and orders for eviction.

"Don't be so glum. Things won't change much for a while." What Lisa means is that neither of us can afford to quit our lives on the outskirts of Houston. We came here for a second chance at love and got stuck. She's promised her father six more months as manager, I've got a new teaching contract to fulfill, and we'll still share meals and the baby, because restaurants and sitters are expensive. We'll keep on like this—two people with little between them except a reluctance to let go.

"You left your cigarettes last night." She hands them to me as I leave. Though we no longer make love, certain nights I bring over some cheap champagne. We put our son to bed together, Lisa nursing him while I stroke back the baby's hair and worry that he isn't completely weaned. In his more frisky moments, Fisher will offer me one of his mother's breasts and laugh. Once he's safely asleep, we turn on the radio and sit in the kitchen. I always make a production of pulling the plastic stopper from the champagne bottle. The little explosion made by the carbonation seems out of place. If I've brought some, we smoke a little grass and move to the living room and cuddle on the couch in front of old movies whose happy endings are never surprises. During commercials, we recount the story of our love. We met as undergraduates at Chapel Hill, where we were both engaged to other people, and in a dorm room we got our first sample of unfaithful love. We use words like *fate* and *destiny* to describe how an Arkansas graduate school re-united us years later. I don't know why, but it soothes me to think that our torn histories are divinely woven. It is as if, until the movie we're watching resumes, we're not divorced.

There is one strange game we play. We get on phones at opposite ends of the apartment, and we talk. Sometimes she reads me poems she has written about the men in her life who have tried to make her happy. We avoid the topics of my drinking and her temper. Often, we talk until first light washes the rooms with its smoky shades of blue. I know this sounds crazy, but I hope it's one of those things she never does with anyone else.

TUESDAY, I baby-sit until it's time to teach. Fisher and I have the gloomy courtyard between the apartment buildings to ourselves. He pokes in the dirt at the base of the gazebo that the workmen never finished. Some steps rise up to where there should be a covered platform, but instead there's nothing. We sit on these steps and admire the finches chattering in the live oaks by the hurricane fence. Today there are fifty or so of them, and Fisher enjoys it when we race toward them and clap our hands and urge them into flight. He likes to gather the fallen feathers and stick them in his hair, and that's what we're doing when a neighbor walks by. She is a beautiful girl of about nineteen with a cardboard box of laundry on her head. She coochie-coos at the baby but avoids eye contact with me. I am simply the manager's husband to these people—a man who is home drinking beer and baby-sitting while his wife collects rents and allows grace periods when they are in arrears.

My neighbor slips into her apartment after much fumbling with keys and locks. All I know about her is that she lives below a couple who have boxing matches some Friday nights and that her boyfriend allows her to admit no one unless he is there. He and Lisa argued over the five extra locks he installed. All the measuring and tightening of screws, the trips to the hardware store and to the locksmith for extra keys—is he keeping harm out or locking his girlfriend in? And the girl: Does she feel safe or like a trapped treasure behind her lover's devices? How do lives get that desperate?

Fisher is bending over, inspecting something at our feet. He squawks because he can't pick it up. I worry that he has found some fire ants. I bend down and can't see anything in the dirt beneath his searching fingers. He looks at his empty hands, puzzled, then grabs again. He is grabbing at our shadows, trying to peel them up and wear them like the feathers we have gathered.

"Mine," he says. "Mine." His word for anything he wants. I stand still so that my shadow will not move, while my son grabs at the airy shape of his father.

WEDNESDAY, THOUGH I have sworn not to, I duck into La Club Mexicana for fortification before teaching. It's the type of bar a sensible person would avoid. The beer is iced down in steel coolers, and the cement floor is gritty with sawdust and cigarette butts. I'm usually the only gringo here and always the only college instructor. The beer is served by beefy Mexican women who will slug a drunk patron who says the wrong thing. The prostitutes scattered at the tables drink their beer Texas-style, in small glasses that can be bumped back like a shot. They have that aged, rough quality young women of their profession get. Everything is spoken in Spanish—a language I don't fully understand— so I drink and grade essays and have no idea of the earnest conversations taking place around me. It's much like drinking in a dream, which is why I come here. The jukebox is full of country-western favorites, like the one about "them old cotton fields back home," sung in Spanish. In a room off the bar, there's a makeshift dance floor with a mirrored ceiling globe, which refracts colored lights in imitation of a high-school prom. When I tire of grading in the poor light, I stand by the room's doorway. Past the curtain of beads, people form couples and dance. As I wave a ten-dollar bill for another drink, a woman misunderstands and walks over and waits awkwardly for me to ask her to dance. Some men at the bar elbow each other and motion their heads toward me. My masculinity is being questioned, so I ask her to dance.

The room is surprisingly spacious, and in the corners and the darkened places along the walls a few couples are groping. All the men have their faces in the breasts of women who stare over the bowed heads bemusedly; it's impossible to guess what they're thinking. The woman I'm with smells of slept-in clothes and cigarettes as she pushes my nose to her neck, whispers something and licks my ear. We slow-dance, and she eases me into a darkened corner. When she massages my stiffness, I bury my face in her cleavage, like the others. She allows me a firm brown breast with a bruised aureole and a pointed nipple. I suckle greedily at the difference between this breast and Lisa's. Then I worry that I'll stain my pants. She unzippers and condoms and masturbates me, her free hand taking the ten from my shirt pocket. Of all the times that I have drunk here, I never thought I would become one of these men in this room.

THURSDAY, SOMETHING strange occurs as I am painting the remaining doors I contracted to paint. I have saved the respectable tenants for last—those near the leasing office. People who look seedy or draw welfare are kept in the back buildings.

Painting a door requires that you stand it open, and in doing so you get a glimpse into all these people's lives. Most of the living rooms are tidy, as if awaiting guests who never arrived. The newly reoccupied ones smell of the carpet deodorizer the cleaning woman uses to remove the scent of pets and previous dwellers. No one is at home, so I am free to appreciate little touches of decoration—an arrangement of handmade flowers set upon a glass coffee table, pictures of family grouped en masse and smiling awkwardly, a coat of arms, velvet cupids and a proudly displayed facsimile of *The Divine Comedy,* which, upon inspection, is a porcelain piggy bank. These rooms are crowded with the kickshaws of the places we call home. I try out sofas and prop my feet on tables. I turn a seascape upside down and wonder who will get the blame. I turn on lights and regroup couch pillows. I search liquor cabinets and help myself to some Wild Turkey, which I drink from someone's favorite juice glass. I haven't done manual labor in a week, and I am one door from finishing when my muscles feel wild with unexpected energy.

The last apartment is the one the management uses for storage. I have forgotten this until I go inside. Law requires that these discarded odds and ends be held in safekeeping for a time. The room smells dank with the things people leave behind. Here are mirrors, boxes of dishes, a few battered stuffed animals, an unstrung bow with some broken arrows, tables with missing legs, broken framed photographs of loved ones. I think that there is nothing I would want to call mine amid this junk when, suddenly, I see the old couch Lisa and I replaced with a newer, larger one. What do you do when you find a part of yourself where you wished you hadn't?

"THE MANAGER IS DIVORCING ME," I letter on the one wall where junk is not stacked. I stand back and admire my work. I repeat the words until they fall apart. I am dancing crazily before them when I feel someone standing at the door. Lisa doesn't say anything, and I hope that this moment and what I've done will be something she never confides to the person who takes my place. Together, we paint over what I have written in this room where no one lives.

ON FRIDAY, Lisa points out that I've been drunk since signing the divorce papers. In a clumsy effort to rekindle her love, I've brought over the ingredients for spaghetti with red clam sauce— her favorite—and there's Chianti, too, and some joints for later.

"Well, let's celebrate my week-long drunk."

She slaps me, hugs the baby and rushes to a neighbor's. While she's gone, I sneak around the apartment. Her diaphragm is in its usual place in her pantie drawer, but who can say if she's used it recently? An inspection of the bedsheets reveals nothing. My suspicions embarrass me.

I am about to smash some pictures of us when I stumble over a jack-in-the-box, which flies open. This is the first toy I ever got my son. The tin contraption fascinates me when played first backward, then forward—how could the same song sound so different? I stand there and put together what I know. I am a man midway through a series of misfortunes—that much I can grasp. I decide to bathe one last time in my old tub and realize, lying with all but my nose underwater, that I will not commit suicide over love. When I put on my clothes again, my socks are stiff and stinking, so I search for a left-behind pair. There seems nothing of mine here until I find a suitcase in the back of the closet.

Inside it are clothes from a time when we still wore each other's jeans and cotton shirts. These are garments still packed from a vacation we once took. Though I am fully dressed, I feel as naked as a baby. I understand that the hope with which these skirts and pants were packed has become irreparably threadbare. I remove a blouse and a skirt. The skirt is made of corduroy— the cloth of kings—and the nap still holds the print of the last time Lisa smoothed it down. Corduroy is something I know about; I put myself through college working summers in a cotton mill that made the fabric. It was in an anthropology class that I met Lisa, but all I can remember of that class is Lisa and the strange fact that in every human language the word for "soul" mimics the sound of an expelled breath.

In the living room, I line up these clothes like people on our couch, and I recollect when we wore them. Then I pick up the skirt and talk to it. I pour us some wine and make promises and then apologize for not keeping those promises. I dance the skirt unashamedly around the room and vow its scent will last forever. I do everything I can do with all that is left of my love except wear it, and, finally, that's what I do. I put that skirt on over my clothes and am admiring its weave when Lisa walks in.

"What are you doing?" she asks. "Have you gone crazy?" My son is asleep in Lisa's arms, so he'll never see his father like this. There's no explaining my actions, so I don't try. I don't even know if Lisa recognizes the skirt as one she once wore. The moment is that uncertain.

I gather the hem of that garment and bring two fistfuls to my nose.

"Smell this," I say. To my amazement, she crosses the room and accepts what I offer her. My ex-wife and I take great gulps of that skirt packed for happier times. We fill our lungs with where we have been.

Corporal Love

I FIRST heard about the types of love in junior high school, when pursed-lipped teachers herded the girls into the library and corralled the boys in the gymnasium so that experts could explain sex. The lecturer—a man about my age now—was the local army recruiter who made extra money terrorizing adolescent audiences with the consequences of Onan's sin (hairy palms and a deterioration of the thought processes) and premarital sex (venereal diseases and Eternal Damnation). His military uniform included a hat neatly tucked and folded along his beltline. He resembled a cross between a scoutmaster and an officer—a lower-level ambassador in the hierarchy of passion.

"Hey, Corporal Love," someone yelled. The name stuck—he didn't seem decorated enough to be a real officer. "Get to the good stuff. Tell us about poontang."

His lecture was supplemented with slides depicting the male and female reproductive organs and a film about the horrors of gonorrhea and syphilis. The diseases didn't scare anyone; penicillin could cure anything, and besides, it took twenty or so years for the spirochetes to crawl up the urinary tract and infect the brain or spinal column. Corporal Love showed the facade of Dix's Hill—the mental asylum for our region of North Carolina—and of the hundred-plus windows, fifteen or so were X-ed over because they housed syphilitically insane patients. At age thirteen, a bed in a room where you were crazy seemed a fair price to pay for twenty years of unmitigated fornication.

After the disappointing slide show (just diagrams, not real genitals) and the film ("Where are the *tits?*" Skeeter Rainy kept yelling. "My dad has films with women who show their tits.") an open discussion followed. Corporal Love invited us to bellow out every name we knew for genitalia. He chuckled and smoked a cigarette thoughtfully. In our junior high, teachers hid in the lounge to smoke, and this unabashed violation of etiquette was exotic. He bet our arsenal of nouns and verbs for sex would be exhausted before he finished his cigarette. He was right.

Then he stormed into a discourse on love. He named the four types: for God and country; between parents and children; the intellectual kind between friends; and the combustible feeling that exists between men and women. Of these, God and country was highest, and he quoted Latin to prove it—*dulce et decorum est pro patria mori.* This was during Vietnam, when men were saying no to that particular commitment. Would we give our bodies for freedom, our blood to stanch the red tide of communism? We all knew he would not unveil door number four until he received a correct answer.

"Yes, Corporal Love," we shouted.

"I can't *hear* you."

"Yes, Sir," we thundered.

We had pleased Corporal Love, and he smiled. He explained carnal love was lowly but necessary. Its function was to build a populace, a nation. He shook his head sadly and prophesied that many of us would become slaves to sexual desire. His message was simple: We should save ourselves for the right woman to marry, but we should be prepared in this holy quest to stumble a time or two. We must pick ourselves up and persevere. God, America, and our future wives required a pure heart. He then spoke of girls who did it, whom we should avoid. Our mission in life was to win the affections of a girl who was of a pure essence. We should marry and worship her. It was spiritual love versus carnal delights, and he made the flesh irresistible.

Three weeks later, on a hunting trip with my father and uncle, my father made a joke about my having found Old Jake. I reddened because he knew why I stayed in the shower long after the hot water ran cold. A doe was strapped to the car's hood; we would eat hunter's fare—backstrap meat with biscuits and gravy—that night. My uncle had recently returned from Vietnam in one piece with stories of communist prostitutes with razors hidden in their vaginas and anecdotes of the pleasures a pack of Winstons would fetch. My father countered with escapades involving Korean women. Then they remembered I was in the backseat and stopped their reminiscing. My uncle decided to pull over and urinate before the old logging road fed into the hard-topped highway. He asked for the time, pulled a pill from his pocket, and washed the capsule down with a Blue Ribbon. My father said he was tired of me snitching beer from the refrigerator and handed me one. My uncle braced both hands on either side of the deer and grunted when the stream finally shot forth.

My father explained his brother had come home with an Asian malady difficult to cure. I explained what Corporal Love had told us about penicillin. My father nodded—not really listening—and contemplated the doe with its little lopsided tongue. He had been distant since my mother left a month before to "visit" a friend. He tossed back another beer and warned me to watch out for the stuff. I didn't know if he meant booze or his and my mother's misfortune or what my uncle had contracted in southeast Asia. I repeated the Corporal's words, *Love's Diseases,* in a silent litany. I reasoned I was immune to them because I wasn't allergic to the cure.

My first love knocked out my front incisor so I could buy her a charm bracelet with the tooth fairy money. She climbed the dogwood which straddled our yards, perched on a limb so that her foot was level with my mouth, and punted. She took out several other baby teeth in the process; we were rich for a week, and she treated me like a wounded hero. I was nine or ten and couldn't understand why her bald biscuit excited such a stiffening when we played doctor. My penis made a little tent of feelings in my shorts. Her eighth-grade sister dated boys with cars. Big sister had explained the mechanics of coupling to Holly, who relayed them to me. These dispatches got garbled in the translation; Holly explained we were supposed to pee on each other. Inside a double-wide playhouse built of refrigerator boxes her brothers had taped together, Holly and I fumbled with the adult concept of union. If I swept the dirt floors and brought bologna sandwiches from home, I got a glimpse of what I would later learn to call her mound of Venus. For a timed minute on her Cinderella watch, Holly allowed me to stroke and kiss something as foreign as the moonscape. *You're so nasty,* she'd say. *Go home now before anyone knows.* When I rounded the corner of her house, her other boyfriend, Monty Sox, ambushed me. If I curled up like an armadillo, he couldn't kick my stomach. Often, Holly would hear us and come watch. Sometimes she'd throw a rock at him or threaten to call her brothers, who smoked cigarettes in front of their parents and threatened the life of a mailman trying to deliver a draft notice.

"You took that beating for me, didn't you?" Holly said. She

called me her champion. "He said dirty things about what we do, so you stood up for my honor." I agreed. All the notions I had about happiness and America would get entangled with this girl-next-door. When they teach you that our country is a woman whose virtue must be protected, what else is a fellow to think?

CERTAIN WEEKENDS when I was eighteen, while Walter Cronkite recapped the Watergate hearings, my father announced it was time for a barbeque and dragged out the grill. Senator Sam's soothing drawl seemed better dining music than the previous year's body counts or race riots. Looking back, my people always took their meals to a backdrop of broadcast misfortune, but of all the woes we broke bread over, none seemed sadder than the lonesomeness of supper in a house love had abandoned. My father sensed this, and if my mother was between boyfriends, he'd phone and coax her over for a family reunion though their divorce was finalized. If she were melancholy and needed propping up, she'd arrive around five. Holly's parents, the Locklears, were invited; my father had started an electrical wiring company with Holly's father, Lamar. Holly's mother, Wanda, and my mother had been high school homecoming queens; they sipped Tab laced with gin and complimented each other on their girlish figures. Glasses clinked as toasts were made to happy times in rented seaside bungalows where we had vacationed together. When the gin was gone some whiskey got opened; the first fire went to ashes and I laid another. Those afternoons, whatever conspiracy my parents had enjoyed somehow surfaced. My father and Lamar raced the car's engine and peeled tires like teenagers as they went to buy steaks.

"He's still in love with me," my mother said once, as the LaSabre fishtailed away. "That's probably the most flattering thing in the world."

"Why don't you love him back?" I asked.

"Oh, Richard," she said, "I do. I'm just not *in* love with him. I hope you never have to know the difference."

Holly and I were engaged by then, and our parents always insisted we drive to the VFW and have a drink. My father commandeered the Harley and drove my mother while I chauffeured the Locklears. Post 349 had a cement dance floor and a brown bag license. People formed couples and danced to "Blue Moon Over Kentucky." When our parents wobbled huffing back to the table, Holly and I made our excuses and our exit. Sometimes, whole groups of couples would gather in the gravel parking lot to admire the Harley's grumbling and talk motorcycle talk before we roared off. Once, someone threw wedding rice from a reception held a few days earlier. Our parents waved as we left, and I could never tell if they were acknowledging what they remembered or what they still believed in.

Holly and I drove through the countryside to a deserted mill village that resembled a ghost town. The houses were gutted shells of themselves, missing panes and sinks and copper tubing. Anything of worth had been confiscated and sold for salvage. It was difficult to imagine people laughing and playing checkers and giving birth in these barren rooms. The deserted village had sidewalks sprouting grass and a church with a condemned sign that resembled a bigger mill house with a steeple. For some superstitious reason, the pews and part of the altar were intact.

Holly presented her virginity to me on the splintery floor of that church. She simply grinned, sat astraddle me, wriggled, and I exploded. After that my catechumenical instruction began. Holly showed me where to touch, what force to use, when to hold back, and when to un-rein. Nothing was forbidden: We tried fellatio in the pulpit, cunnilingus in the choir box, dorsal commingling before the altar. Our moans and gasps congregated in the empty corners and came back at us as the oldest of cantatas. The roof had a hole from wind damage, and lying beside Holly after love, looking up into the evening's first stars, I'd physically shudder. Holly would make the joke about someone walking over my grave and we'd make love again and have our laugh at time. Then we'd talk about our future after I went to college, the house we'd buy, and the names we would give our children.

This was in 1973.

MY NEXT engagement was ten years later to Felice. I was nearly thirty and had spent my twenties on relationships with a string of dancers. The first graduate school I quit boasted a dance department with a building of mirrored rooms where women in tights fought gravity to hang suspended in space. My forays were more earthbound. I jumped from a first-story bedroom window when Sharon's boyfriend surprised us on Halloween, got dumped by Vanessa for a female potter whose hands knew shapes. Once, I woke up bound to a bed while a woman in a merry widow painted my toenails. The soaring love I promised each of these women crashed. The casualties mounted, and I became a veteran of such skirmishes.

Watch the evening news—disasters must be reported calmly. I slugged Felice once, during a lover's argument, as she was beating on me and screaming that I would *not* ignore her. When I hit her, it seemed like slow motion. She ran into the bedroom and called 911. Our apartment was in a converted Victorian house, and though she had locked the bedroom door, the phone jack was in the hall. When I unplugged it, her threats became serious. I wondered, would our neighbors ignore us as we did them when they fought? Prostrate before the locked door, I begged forgiveness. I was the essence of a batterer.

We sought help from a therapist who specialized in domestic disharmony. She smoked more than I did, and she openly flirted with me. This therapist lit my cigarettes and asked for details of my sex habits and fantasies. When Felice piped up, she'd cut her short.

"It's probably just part of the counseling process," I told Felice as she complained on the way home from our third and last visit. We both had been accepted to graduate schools in different states, and were plotting escapes.

In addition to the couples therapist, Felice visited a psychiatrist weekly and an abortionist once. I had wanted the baby, but there were careers to consider. Back home in bed after the abortion, I held Felice, feeling guilty for wanting to make love yet wondering when we could. I reasoned the act of physical commingling might carry us past the truth that our life together was ending.

I NEVER hit a woman again, though I plotted ways to kill a man to protect the woman I would marry, Lisa, after she waltzed into my life again.

The guy she dated before me was a stalker. When Lisa first moved into my apartment, he'd call and claim he was watching us both, then hang up. He added a desperado quality to our love. On his crazier days, he made threats from my parking lot on one of the first car phones in Arkansas. He seemed to want phone warfare, so I retaliated. I called the utility companies, pretending to be him and said I was moving to Alaska. His services were stopped. We switched to an unlisted number when his phone was reconnected. Lisa and I were finishing graduate school together, and he began prowling the halls like an echo, bouncing back and startling us. He frequented the pool hall where I drank beer, sat on a stool next to me, and smiled as he twiddled his thumbs. I had friends in the pool hall who would, if I asked, rough him up. The owner slipped me a napkin with the number of a man who remedied such problems for fifty bucks, and I seriously considered protecting my love for Lisa in this fashion.

"Piece of advice, pal," I said to the stalker once. I waved to the
bartender that things were all right. "You and Lisa just weren't
meant to be. Besides, you can't lose what you never had. You better remember that."

Then he said he would kill us.

When Lisa and I got married, he changed tactics. He'd appear
in parking lots—a grinning face behind a windshield. His
bumper followed a foot from my thigh as we lugged groceries to
our car. Evenings when we walked in the deserted stillness of an
old graveyard, he'd rocket through and laugh as we scattered into
the headstones. We moved to an old hunting cottage on top of
a mountain, reasoning you had to be lost to find your way there.
The district attorney with whom we filed twenty-nine complaints of harassment explained bodily injury had to occur.

By then Lisa was pregnant, *sacred,* full of figure and of what
our love had begat. The stalker never found us on that mountain;
I heard he threw a log through another girlfriend's window when
they broke up.

It's strange, but as the due date neared, I became convinced
this guy was biding his time like some pestilence. Surely, he was
waiting to kill us in our sleep. Nights after making love, while
Lisa slept, I sat on the front porch protecting my family from him
and other uncertainties. Sipping whiskey, I formulated what I'd
do if he were luckless enough to stumble upon our house and
cross the threshold I had carried Lisa over. Twice I got out an old
double-barreled sixteen-gauge shotgun issued by the Army in
WWI. I set a box of buckshot by my feet and jumped when box
turtles or deer rustled the leaves in our garden. Who knows
what I would have done if he had showed up. I'd like to think I
could have talked him into leaving, or that my aim would have
guided the buckshot whistling past his ear, frightening him into
running. Then again, there's the part of me that *wanted* him to
cross over the mark separating loved ones and invited guests

from burglars and thieves. That part of me wanted to lay waste to his heart.

My marriage to Lisa lasted three years and relocation into as many states. I hauled us to lectureship appointments at community colleges. We had our son in Arkansas and spoke openly of endings in Mississippi. We tried to rekindle our relationship in Texas, the state which stamped its seal on our divorce decree. We loved each other—often noisily—and for that I am grateful. Those years were so much like other people's attempts at love that it's easy to chart an image of them. One essay I now teach, written by a famous psychologist, insists we each carry around a love map—a sketchy cartography formed in childhood which outlines the topography of the people to whom we will surrender our hearts. I told this to Lisa once, when she had strewn my clothes like police body outlines across the front lawn.

"If that's the case," she said, "your love map looks like a battlefield."

This was during the divide and conquer stage of our divorce. Our strife has given way to seasonal reunions much like my parents', when the weather along the White River in Arkansas is accommodating or at least forgiving. Lisa and I live three states apart, and we rendezvous at a campsite miles upstream from the real estate scandal. The last time we spent the night, Lisa was en route from Little Rock, where she teaches, to Oklahoma, where her significant other lived. Our son and I would head back to North Carolina for a few weeks.

While Lisa was on the car phone explaining this spur of the moment camping trip to the man who would take my place, I pitched the tent. The guy had none of my unreasonable qualities and asked would I send him some trout if we caught enough. We pitched camp and Lisa claimed first rights to the hammock.

I took our son wade fishing. A few hundred yards downriver

from the campsite, I imagined us a family on one of the world's earliest evenings. We seemed exiles from the little routs that rule mankind. I hooked a fat rainbow and steadied my son in the current as I gave him the rod to fight the fish. He asked me where did the fish's colors go after I had gutted and gilled it. I didn't know what to say, so I named what I knew of the appearing stars and hoisted him on my back with supper in tow. Fathers don't like to be ignorant of things, especially the heavens, so I manufactured names for the configurations I didn't know. I *did* get Venus right, though my son remarked the evening star looked like a beacon that warns planes of the earth's proximity. I thought of all the names he would know love by—from his mother's to mine to the stranger he would marry to the sounds by which they would know their children.

That night we ate the first trout my son ever battled. Though it was July, we built a fire, and I told him stories of the first time I had ever seen his mother. I put in all the true clichés about my knees going akimbo and my crazy habit of going into a room Lisa had left to inhale the perfume of where she had been. Our son fell asleep as if I were telling him a fairy tale.

"If I didn't know you any better, I'd think you believed in that stuff." Lisa had returned from carrying our son inside the tent, and she stood at the firelight's edge, part shadow, part real. When she came over to grab a cigarette from my pocket, she shrugged—she was trying to quit—and lit it with a smoldering stick. I poured us bourbon as she smoked thoughtfully. I knew her well enough not to speak and to guess what she was deciding. When she said we should go into the tent but be *quiet* about it, I followed.

"That's the last time we'll do that," she said when we finished.

Lying beside her in our aftermath, I lifted up my hand to test its strength in the tent's shadowy light. I wished for all of us whatever solace a hand raised in salutation could offer. This hand had admired breasts and traced iliac crests and caught a son and cut his umbilical cord. It had hit, and it had shut my father's eyes on his deathbed. It had pointed fingers in accusation and shushed away fears; it had worn rings and flung them away. This hand was no stranger to love's hierarchy of feelings. I remembered Corporal Love waving good-bye that day, admonishing us to be good soldiers with pure hearts, and my father's laugh when he admitted that in his service days he had fallen victim to love's diseases. Then Lisa's hand rose up to meet mine—she didn't know what I was thinking, but she knew it was time for a laying on of hands. We did that children's trick and chanted *here's the church, here's the steeple, open the doors, and there's all the people.* Our son whimpered in his sleep, and we brought him between us and stroked his hair. When I touched Lisa's face and neck—not in a sexual way this time because we had gone past where the body matters—her features felt like my own and yet someone else's. Then Lisa curled around our son and slept, and like a foot soldier, I held watch over their sleeping beauty. I knew that to doze would break the spell of what I was feeling. The chittering of birds outside finally reminded me I had promised Lisa and our son a breakfast of hashbrowns and trout prepared Scottish style. I would have to muster my stiff bones soon, but for a while longer I lingered, adoring them, in love with these people, and the grace of this borrowed moment, and the imperfection of things which pass.

What We Are Up Against

MY FATHER died obsessed with being remembered. His tombstone was a granite reproduction of Winged Victory engraved with *Think of me as you pass by / As I am, soon will you lie.* Years earlier, when I was eight, he had brought home a monument catalog and proudly pointed out his choice to my mother. The headstone idea had come from one of the many art correspondence courses he received mail-order.

"I refuse to be buried beside you under a woman with no head," my mother had said.

"This thing has class," he had claimed.

"Over my dead body."

"Don't tempt me."

When they divorced, I was an adolescent and still a runt. Saturdays, my father instructed me in the delicate art of falling. We drove the company truck to a public swimming pool with a high dive which he taught me to perform from, though he never ventured up the diving board himself. Instead he stood at the edge of the pool, his thick arms angled across his chest so that his mermaid tattoo showed. I learned flips and full gainers and jack-knives, imagining I was falling not into the water but into that woman on his arm. He had got the tattoo in the Navy—before I was born—and she seemed proof that my father had and could lead lives other than the one we were quitting. He had been a hospital supply salesman, co-owner of a struggling electrical construction company, and finally director of special projects for the county hospital—all before my voice could give this full account to my memory of him. When we finished swimming, he sometimes drank too much and claimed that he and I once flew together.

"I fixed that cropduster's engine, and up we went into the wild blue yonder. You remember that day?"

I didn't.

His ability to repair almost anything except his marriage was very real, and it landed him the special projects director job in our section of North Carolina where nearly everyone worked in textiles. He married my mother—a small-town beauty who was highly nervous—out of his genuine need to fix things. He promised her the moon but couldn't deliver it, and she divorced him because he failed to secure a better position in a more exciting part of the country. I have since decided that geography played a part in their undoing. Both my parents lived and died in an unremarkable section east of Greensboro, along the fall line, where the land forgets the Appalachians as it relaxes into the piney straightness of the coastal plain, and where the landscape easily recovers from any small marks made upon it.

Not until my own divorce did I understand the unmoored feeling my father must have been up against during certain moments in his life. I had forgotten about the mermaid and about what living alone in the Piedmont of North Carolina could do to a person when he called one night a year before his death to complain that his tattoo was fading. He usually called after bourbon had made him reminiscent and melancholy.

"I'm sorry to hear Miss Clairol's not what she used to be," I said. My father had named the mermaid after the Clairol lady who seductively shook free her hair on the old commercials.

"Hey," he said. "I think I'll get another one right on top of the old one."

"That's a good idea."

"Damned right," my father said. "I'll go to the grave with that woman on my arm."

"You're a little drunk, aren't you?" In the background an announcer listed arrivals and departures and boarding times. My father liked to drink in airport bars.

"Hey," he said. "You and Fisher still coming next weekend?"

"About that trip," I said. I didn't know how much influence I wanted my father to exert over my son; most of our father-son-grandson trips had ended in calamity. "I think the trip might be off. In fact," I lied, "Lisa has been reluctant to give me custody of Fisher for the trip."

"I straightened her out. I called about an hour ago, and she said she thought the trip would be good for Fisher. I think she wants him out of her hair for the weekend."

"The truth is," I tried to say.

"The truth is you sound like hell, and you need a little vacation. C. Chaplin will meet you boys at the airport with a surprise." He hung up.

C. Chaplin was the alias my father gave all travelers who asked when he drank in airport bars. "Sit here with old C. Chaplin and have a drink while you tell about where you're headed. I'm stuck here too." There amidst delayed flights and missed connections, my father swapped his life of floor plans and building codes for that of an elderly and genial businessman snagged by a layover.

He usually carried a briefcase and wore his plaid hat with the cropped feather on these occasions, and he always stood the rounds. The kinder travelers he met sent back postcards to C. Chaplin, wishing him luck in his freight empire or his oil ventures or his dental hygiene supply company. C. Chaplin had as many occupations as my father's imagination could muster, and his office in the hospital's boiler room was wallpapered with the greetings they sent. My father got an impish pleasure from designing critical care units and helicopter pads while surrounded by all the different ways he would be remembered. C. Chaplin was the part of my father which actually *liked* the way airport bars are architectured to mimic something familiar from the lives those in transit left behind.

THE SURPRISE my father had manufactured was a night of camping complete with two women named Sal and June whom he had befriended with bourbons as he waited for our delayed flight to arrive. Sal had won an airline sweepstakes which included free tickets for two for a whole month anywhere in the continental United States. They had visited sixteen states besides their native Tennessee, and were touring North Carolina with the one thousand free rental miles which came with the grand prize. My father had persuaded them to form a camping caravan with us. He steered Fisher and me from our arrival gate to the airport bar where two tired women of about thirty-six sat. Sal was a tall woman with stooped shoulders from trying to look shorter. She had horsy features and crowded teeth. She wore a Virginia-Is-For-Lovers T-shirt and a Visit-The-Great-Smokey-Mountains beaded belt. June was her counterpart, but proportioned and much shorter. As they dressed alike, I got the impression of seeing double but out of focus. They already knew my name was Richard and that Fisher liked swimming, and that bothered me.

"So we're all going camping," June said. "Hey. When you travel with a nutty and impulsive gal like Sal, anything can happen."

Sal remarked that if you had told her this morning she would meet a man named C. Chaplin in an airport bar, and he would talk her into doing something like this, she would have told you that you were crazy.

"This is ludicrous," I told my father when they had excused themselves to use the bathroom.

"Hubba, hubba," my father said. "We've got two live wires."

"What's live wires?" asked Fisher.

"Hot to touch," explained my father.

"Dad, are those two women yours and Grandad's girlfriends?"

"No. Here." I gave Fisher my calling card. "Run out to those phones and call your mother and tell her we've arrived safely." When Fisher left, I said to my father, "Get rid of them." I hurried to the noisy phoning area.

"Mom, the plane didn't crash or anything. We just had two layovers. Travelers *expect* things like that." Fisher rolled his eyes at me. "And guess what, Mom, we're going camping at a place where they have extraterrestrials." My father had promised Fisher that Crater Lake was frequented by men from space. "Visit Crater Lake," Fisher read from the brochure. "The only lake proven to have been formed from a meteor's impact. This lake dates back to the cataclysm which extinguished the dinosaurs. Isn't that neat?" As he listened, he tugged at the metal extension cord to test its strength. "Mom, of course I love you." Then he said, "Here, she wants to *discuss* something with you."

I covered the receiver, told Fisher to go sit in the bar with his grandfather. "Hello," I said to Lisa. "It seems we're going to camp and hunt for spacemen."

"Richard, you have to do something about your father."

I misunderstood, and in an instant I had confessed that under no circumstances was I going camping with two prostitutes.

"You kill me," she said. "You'll invent anything to make me jealous. Well, it's not working."

"Well, what's so strange about taking a kid on a wild-goose chase?" I reminded her that each trip back, my father cooked up some crazy expedition to please Fisher.

"I don't mean that."

"Did another bundle of those bird pictures arrive?" In the years after my parents' divorce, my father mourned his lost marriage by painting some sixty pictures of birds. Then, in fear of his own death, he sent them in carefully wrapped packages to Fisher as keepsakes.

"It's worse than those paintings," Lisa said. "Today he called twice and just hung up. I knew it was him because there were airport noises in the background, and every time you and I visited, he'd been tooting it up in the airport bar all morning. Get him to stop. It sounds awful, like someone trying to say something when they can't."

"I miss you," I said to change the subject. I stood there wondering why her voice had such an effect on me while two booths down a man hurriedly explained that he would explain when he got home.

"Richard, don't start that."

I said that the last time I called, some stranger could be heard singing in my bathroom.

"It's neither your bathroom nor your business."

"And I'm sorry if my father calls at the wrong time and *interrupts* something."

"And I hope that you children find what you're looking for." She slammed down her receiver. Two booths down, the man who wanted to explain when he got home had changed tactics. He threatened to search her out wherever she went and steal her back. My reflection in the pay phone's cover was *not* that of a man who kicked doors in to reclaim love. Instead, I resembled a puzzled traveler at baggage claims who had just been told his suitcase was en route to a foreign country. Such people always had helpless looks on their faces, and I wondered how long Lisa had seen me like that.

SAL SAT in the back of the van with Fisher, helping him rummage through the stockpile of tents and sleeping bags and tins of beans and franks and the celestial map with the constellations in their late-summer order—everything my father considered necessary for a night under the stars in search of visitors from outer space.

"This is like Camp Fire Girls," Sal sniffled. "I had a rotten childhood, but I was a campfire girl for a summer." At least she had stopped crying. When I had returned from calling Lisa, Sal and June were quarreling over renting a small truck or a sports car. They had argued like a married couple. June yelled that Miss Sweepstakes Winner had made all of the decisions from day one of the trip. Sal claimed June was a loser who never won anything. When I suggested that we had to go, but that my father would set them up for as many drinks as they liked, they joined forces against me.

"He thinks we're cheap," one said.

"He doesn't think we're good enough to go along," the other said.

Fisher started crying. "Dad," he pointed to the brochure, "you can rent boats here, and Sal promised to teach me to ski. Now I'll never learn."

"I consider you responsible for all of this," I had whispered to my father as we piled into his van. Now we were speeding through airport traffic with June in a sports car behind us, honking that we go faster.

"For God's sake let her pass you," I said to my father.

"That's why I wouldn't ride with her," said Sal.

I felt for the bottle under my father's seat and poured bourbon into my coffee. I was a man officially divorced but still worrying how I would explain any of this weekend to Lisa. We had usually talked in bed, and I imagined her fingertips drumming on my stomach as she remarked that the situation was sad, not funny. I heard her say two half-drunk grown men with a child in their care chasing tarts, and I had another drink of bourbon on that one. A third slug of bourbon convinced me I was probably better off divorced. Then I remembered once when I had tried to explain to Lisa why my own parents had split up. She and I were newlyweds in bed happily confiding things. Lisa had insisted *something* caused the divorce. All I could think to say was that my mother saw my father as a loser. I explained that during the last year of their marriage, my father had begun building home improvements with a vengeance—as if increasing the value of his property might save his marriage. We rescreened the porch, we built a brick patio, we poured a concrete driveway and planted privet along its border. None of this pleased my mother, and each afternoon she sat chain-smoking beside a window and listened to our hammers, ringing. I had explained to Lisa that my parents' last fight occurred one Friday when my father came home from work and got the feist so excited it wet on the welcome mat. My mother usually thought this was funny, but that day she screamed she would kill herself rather than sleep one more night with him. My father carried the feist from the mat to the couch and held it there while it still urinated. After he put down the dog, my mother slapped him. That night he drank on his patio with his back to the house. He sat there past night into dawn. He drank from the bottle and made chirping noises when the blue jays and the wrens flocked to his feeder at first light. By dawn he was very drunk and singing, his voice off-key and full of the ache of things which can no longer be maintained. Somehow I couldn't tell Lisa that he had sung, because your father drunk and singing after your mother has locked him from the house is a private memory too easily misinterpreted. A listener might think you divined something about your own marriage in the incident.

SAL DECIDED we should play Camp Fire Girls as we neared Crater lake. "You know, tell stories like they do around campfires." Fisher said he didn't know any stories, but he bet he could ski on the first try. My father asked had he ever told the story of our first airplane ride.

"About a hundred times," said Fisher.

"Ladies first," said Sal. She told us about the places she had flown. Fisher kept insisting she tell us something about skiing—how had she learned?

"My first husband, Thurmon, taught me that." She said they had honeymooned at Niagara Falls in a cottage so close to the precipice that the water going over sounded like someone gone crazy on the kettle drums. "We had to leave because I got depressed. All that water made so much noise we had to yell to hear each other, and I guess we got used to yelling because we never stopped." She poured more bourbon into the top of her Coke bottle, stoppered it with her thumb and shook, and turned philosophical after a few sips. She claimed us all like a happy family in the late movies heading toward a quaint vacation. "And all because Mr. Chaplin here was nervous about your visit, and he ducked into a bar to steady his nerves, and he started talking to us. Isn't life strange?"

"Certain days sure as hell are." I frowned at my father.

"Richard," Sal said. "Your father thinks you don't like him."

I barked something about her being a drunken Ann Landers, and she started crying again.

"Here, now, we're supposed to be having a *good* time," said my father. *"I've* got something to tell," and he launched into the story of our first airplane ride.

"I took this guy up once when he was a kid." He pointed his head at me. "The carburetor wouldn't work, so the cropduster wouldn't start. I had the thing off in five minutes and adjusted the floats. The pilot wanted to take the thing up alone, to see if it was really fixed, but I said, 'Hell, I know the thing won't conk out,' and away we went into the wild blue yonder."

Now my father simply imagined this plane ride; he and I never flew together in an airplane, just as we never remembered the same things. Yet as he told the story of our ten-dollar aerial tour of Alamance County, it *became* my memory. I saw myself as a snotty-nosed kid growing out of a crew cut, amazed at being airborne with his father on an otherwise uneventful Sunday. When my father claimed to Sal and Fisher that he had slipped the pilot an extra five bucks to do a loop that day, my hands actually sweated as I imagined that boy beside his father, free of gravity and upside down. I imagined him saying he and my mother simply grew apart, as if so high above the surface of where we lived the concept of distances could be truly appreciated. My father explained that my mother had promised to strew the backyard with sheets—fourteen of them which spelled HI!—and she didn't. He claimed it was impossible to locate our house from all the others in the county.

"That was some Sunday morning, huh, Richard?"

"Sure," I said, but the Sunday morning I remembered was the long, earthbound drive back to graduate school, when I felt divided between my parents. Specifically, I remembered the Sunday morning awkwardness of two men trying to shave in a too-small bathroom mirror the morning after he and Lisa had argued over something inconsequential—how to make a perfect Manhattan. She had gotten angry and driven back to Arkansas, leaving me to weather the weekend and to explain to my father that she and I were, in fact, *already* married, and that my mother had witnessed at the Justice of the Peace's office on the sole condition that we not invite my father. I remembered listening to Lisa and my father argue as the ice for the perfect Manhattan melted in my hands, realizing how she and I sounded when *we* argued. Later, during a fight, she screamed that I was becoming so much like my father in looks and deeds that it made her skin *loathe*. It was the way she used "loathe" that made me walk from the house that morning and not return, and that night in a Ramada Inn I had dreamed Fisher and myself in my father's plane, and there in my yard was not HI! but LOATHE! written in my bedsheets. I couldn't sleep after the dream, so I sat smoking until my gums ached and my mouth tasted of pennies. I counted every way I had ever had Lisa. Then I called but hung up when she answered. I found myself thinking of a time when I was twenty. I had helped my father move. He had converted a spare bedroom into a makeshift studio and an old stepladder into an easel. In the five years he had lived there, he had filled canvas upon canvas with different birds—all with the head of my mother. In each, she was young with wild, raven hair and sleepy eyes. His paintings resembled something ancient people both feared and worshiped.

"What's this?" I had asked. My father shrugged and sheepishly began to wrap and stack them. I hadn't seen him blush in years. Along the walls and shelves of the studio, placed like decoys, were paintings of every bird of passage I could imagine, each with my mother's early-morning look in which she seemed someone wandering through a garden after waking from a dream. I stood there in the middle of my father's odd ornithological tribute to the creatures who inhabit the place where love goes, not knowing what to say. It saddened me to imagine all the sleepless nights my father must have spent at the stepladder's bottom, trying to get her image just right. When he had wrapped enough for an armful, I carried them to the U-Haul. The moment was one of those awkward ones when you turn from someone's hurt because it reminds you of your own.

CRATER LAKE boasted ultramodern camping facilities, an amusement park featuring a carnival that weekend, and ski boat rentals. June had beaten us there by fifteen minutes and had reserved us a campsite.

"Hey," the attendant said happily. "You guys must be the Chaplin party."

My father mumbled something and signed the register.

"The name's not Chaplin," I said.

"Whatever," the attendant said. "We don't ask questions here. All I know is that a certain June said I should be expecting you. Y'all got campsite 118." Then he said two congregations of Baptists were using the lake to get baptized, but that he had stuck us as far away from them as possible. He winked.

We stopped at the bathhouse to change, then went to our campsite. Campsite 118 was a stretch of packed dirt under a strand of white oaks which were covered with poison oak. Queen Anne's lace grew from the dirt's edge to a manmade beach which bordered the lake. I cautioned Fisher about chiggers and poison oak and showed him how to pitch the tents while my father sat at the picnic table with Sal and June and explained how he had got his tattoo. Sal came over with a bourbon my father had mixed for me. She wore a bathing suit and caught me looking at a purple bruise on her thigh.

"It's not from what you think," she said.

"I don't care how you got it."

"Drink your drink like a good little boy." When she walked back to the picnic table, she asked my father to rub suntan lotion into her back. He used both hands.

"Ski time!" he yelled when he had finished. He went to the waterfront to rent a boat and ski equipment. The bourbon and the good smell of freshly unfolded canvas made me forget Sal and June for a moment. I raised the first tent's ridgepole with my son, and stood back enjoying the plunking sound of his hatchet hammering home the stakes. The bright lake made me squint. Across the water's surface, skiers hung suspended and caught in the drowsy stages of skiing. One boat tried to raise a skier, while a fisherman shook an angry fist at a teenager on a slalom course who had sprayed him. Another boat swung back to recast the rope to a fallen skier. On the lake's opposite side, figures in robes awaited their turn at immersion. The crowd's hymn was lost across the distance, and they went into the water two by two where men with dark suits received them. I imagined that the cool water and the minister's large hand pushing me under could make a difference. Then I found myself yearning for something as simple as a slippery shower with a woman I had no history with. I wanted a quiet moment with no noise to shout over. On our side of the lake a plump woman with a bathing cap was walking from the water.

"Hey," Sal yelled. "Does he know how to ski?" She pointed at my father walking toward us in the deliberate fashion of men who wish not to stumble from a day's drinking. Her question seemed something I should know, but didn't, and I was ashamed. He wore shorts, and his legs made me understand why old men prefer long pants—even on beaches.

"Let me try the skis first," I said to my father.

"*I'll* show everyone how it's done," my father said. There was nothing to do but let him try it. We decided June and Fisher would watch from the bank while Sal and I tried to get my father up.

"Hit it!" my father yelled once everything was situated. I gunned the motor and felt the heavy, planetary feel of my father in tow. I dragged him some seventy-five yards with the top of his head periscoping the lake's surface. I kept thinking, *Let go, damn it, let go.* I feared he would pull loose the boat's transom. Finally, he let go of the ski rope, and when I swung the boat around to get him, he was sputtering water and coughing. Sal had to help me pull him into the boat. Once in, he lay there groaning.

"I think he's *dying*," she shrieked. She began pumping his stomach as he gasped at great gulps of air. "Somebody has to *do* something." Then she tilted his head back and gave him mouth to mouth. A second after she began breathing into him, she shrieked again. "My God," she said, and then she spat and slapped him. My father slipping Sal his tongue seemed the funniest thing he had ever done, but when I laughed she slapped me too.

"I thought you liked me," my father said.

"You old fool," she said. "You disgust me." She spat again to show her disgust.

"And you." She turned on me. "I feel sorry for you and the way you wear your hurt around like some damned merit badge. Take me back to shore before I drown you both."

SAL AND June spent the afternoon complaining to two campers at site 120 that they had practically saved a man's life only to have him molest Sal. My father raised his glass of bourbon in salute each time Sal or June pointed exasperatedly our way. Campsite 120 consisted of two college boys who said they were from Syracuse when they marched over to claim Sal's and June's overnight bags. They kept referring to the incident as a "messy situation."

"We don't want this potentially messy situation to escalate," said the spokesman. His friend slammed the door on Sal's rented sports car and sat inside with the engine idling. "You see," the spokesman said, "we're Kappa Sigs and we like to leave a good impression wherever we go. The women, they like prefer our company, so we came to get their stuff."

"Yeah." The friend craned his head out the window. "It's our turn with them now. You guys blew your chance."

"This isn't like musical chairs or a pass-around bag of popcorn." My father's glass tinkled against a rock as he sat it down, and he struggled to raise himself from the lawn chair. "You guys aren't gentlemen. You're little snits. Richard, which one do you want me to hit first," and then my father passed out.

"Allow me to apologize for him." I laughed a weak, nervous laugh.

"We're not little snits. We're Kappa Sigs."

"You're absolutely right," I said. "And forget about him. He's dead to the world. He's passed out cold. Why, I bet you won't hear another peep from him until morning." I had gathered Sal's and June's belongings and was placing them in the spokesman's arms.

"Do you need the tent too?" I asked. "I'll take it down for you."

"Whose is it?"

"Either Sal or June rented it. I get them mixed up."

"Sal's the lucky one."

"Right." I was pulling out tent stakes.

"I'd like to ask a favor," the spokesman said. "Pretend we forgot the tent. It might make sleeping arrangements cozier back at our campsite." He walked toward his friend in the sports car. Suddenly I felt enormously old watching the bounce in his step.

TO SAVE what seemed a disastrous day, I left my father sleeping and took Fisher to Crater Lake's amusement center where a carnival was in progress. In my time carnivals had been week-long affairs held in converted pastures strewn with straw and the earthy smells and grunts of agricultural exhibits, but this one resembled the kind set up quickly in the asphalt parking lots of shopping centers. Yet I was amazed at the way carnivals had changed but stayed the same. The freak show didn't have a geek to bite the heads off live chickens, or a reptile woman, or even a two-headed goat, but it *did* have a tattooed lady and a man lying on a board in a coma. For three dollars you could holler into his ear and tickle him with a feather to try to disrupt his otherworldly slumber. I figured his coma was a hoax, but I wondered what that man was dreaming.

I paid three bucks so that Fisher could tickle the man, and it became as if he were tickling me, trying to get me to see things clearly. I stood there putting together what I knew. The source of trouble—the exact moment that had finished us—eluded me. Was it when I had accused Lisa of infidelity; was it when she pitched a bourbon in my face and called me a lousy lover and even worse provider; how had we gotten to the point where door locks got changed and lawyers drew up settlements? What I remembered most as Fisher tried to wake that comatose man was an argument in which a rocking horse landed in my hands. It flew through the picture window like a winged dream. With a shard of glass, I had sliced across the lines in my palm to demonstrate how close we were to *real* violence. After the bandaging, we had made love like teenagers on the kitchen floor, knowing I would have to leave that night. This knowledge made us linger, and Lisa had taken the cigarette from my hand and said she would probably start smoking again. She lit one cigarette with the butt of another, and by the third one, she giggled and showed me smoke rings. She had never done this before. I could have lain forever on the cool linoleum watching this strange, new woman, but we had said the type of things that couldn't be retracted.

"Dad, I tried everything, but I couldn't wake him," said Fisher. I bought him some cotton candy to ease his disappointment. He had never eaten any before, and his face broke with astonishment as he got his first taste of a confection so sugary disappearing into air. I bought beehive after beehive of the stuff, sitting with my son on a bench someone would take down Sunday night. We watched people be people as they can only be at carnivals. We did everything we weren't supposed to do. We laughed when an angry father swatted his daughter a quick one on the tail, we pointed at fat people, we watched when one man dropped his wallet and did not intervene when a watchful adolescent swooped it up and ran away. I was a happy conspirator with my son. We washed down the whole scene with big gulps of grape snow cones served in conical cups. Most of the carnival workers had some type of scar or deformity—a misshapen arm or a long abdominal scar or some of the digits of a hand abbreviated or entirely missing. Fisher asked what kind of people these were, how did they get here. I explained that they were carnival people, that they passed through and set things up like this from place to place. The thought occurred to me that for my son it was as if each time he slept and awoke, some strange and mischievous force was rearranging the shape of things.

"Come on," I said to my boy. We bought two tickets and waited our turn. The day flushed against the horizon as we sat side by side in the Ferris wheel. You can't ride a Ferris wheel without feeling like a kid, and you can't help the way your heart pounds as you rise above the other rides and the lights blinking on here and there as you look down on top of things. As we rounded that point where the upward motion stopped and for one precarious moment we were hung sweetly in balance, I wondered what my son would remember of this instant of perfect stasis.

THOUGH WE sighted no men from outer space, later that night at Crater Lake we witnessed a meteor shower. When we returned from the carnival, my father insisted we take the boat out to Crater Lake's middle. He assured Fisher that spacemen liked to spirit away people in boats on deserted lakes. We sped to Crater Lake's center and drifted, three generations afloat on the shifting surface of a lake formed by a heavenly catastrophe. Fisher dozed, and for a while my father and I said nothing and sipped our drinks.

"He won't be too hurt by all this," my father said finally. "I used to worry that I had somehow hurt you. I used to worry about you skiing with strangers, about not being there if the rope snapped or the boat ran over you."

"Did you ever call Mother up after the divorce and hang up without saying anything?" I asked.

"A few times."

"Hey." I roused Fisher. "You've never seen your old man ski, have you?"

"Dad. It's nighttime. And you can't ski with long pants."

"Who said anything about pants." I began shedding my clothes.

My father was just drunk enough to think this might be funny. "I'll pull you close enough to the bank so's you can moon those featherweights who stole our girls." We were building a day my son would remember.

I did the back dive my father had taught me. I arched into water holding streaks of shooting stars and a lover's moon and pierced through this into darkness. I surfaced sputtering and caught the rope my father threw. He eased the Evinrude into gear with the easiness of a man who respected the things we construct which give us motion. He made Fisher sit in his lap. When the rope pulled tight enough to shake off water, my father gunned the motor.

Soon we were speeding across the lake's surface. I stayed inside the wake to relearn the delicate footing night skiing required.

Then I eased across the mound of water into the clean feel the concave ski produced when it grabbed the smooth water it was fashioned for. The night air tickled and tingled my parts. I swung back and down until my chest ached with my fight to change directions.

"Jump the wake," my father yelled. Fisher screamed Lisa wouldn't like us doing this. My father shouted that we simply wouldn't tell her. "Woo-haw, this is the goddamned life," he bellowed. The stars lay caught in their suddenly perceptible movements, and I leaned against the good feeling the rope made when it was stretched so taut that it sang. When rope sings—this was how I felt. My father gave the motor full power, and he and Fisher began mouthing something inaudible over the distance, but their noise was of motion and the sheer racket things make in their quick passing. On the banks a pointing crowd had gathered. I began to yell too, emptying myself like a kid let loose on a playground. I yelled until my lungs ached, wondering what they would think of the absurd sight of a man pushing middle age, skiing by as naked as the day he was born.

LATER THAT night, while my father snored and Fisher kicked his covers, I made my last phone call. I snuck down the dirt path to the phone booth, and Lisa answered on the ninth ring. Her voice was syrupy with sleep and dreams.

"What, who *is* this? Is anything the matter?" she said. I couldn't answer. "Why are you doing this?" She called me my father's name, and when I hung up I felt like a thief.

All the way back to the tent, I asked myself questions which had no simple answers. Was Lisa awake in the dark, unable to sleep for fear that something awful was about to precipitate? I hoped so, then felt guilty. Each time I had called and said nothing, I had felt telephone close but miles apart—a feeling I never got when I called and said my name and we argued. It was as if there were two of me—the man who loved her and the man who called to hear her husky voice churn into fear. I wondered which man to trust. Then I kicked at a rock along the path because I couldn't answer questions like these, and because I knew I would never have to call her again and not answer. I took off my shoes and grabbed at the dirt with my toes and stopped to listen to the crickets, a man alone along the fall line, empty of answers but amazed at the way the crickets rasped against the edge to the air which promised a change of seasons soon.

That night, I sat outside the tent sipping bourbon from the bottle like my father. I wondered what I would tell Fisher when he came to me and asked of his father the things a son should know. All I knew to explain to my son was that once, when I was twenty, my father had insisted that he and I visit the graveyard where his tombstone—the one ordered years earlier on installments—had finally been set into place. The odd thing was that starlings were flocking there that day, looping and funneling down to carpet the cemetery in a living tide. The lawn was thick and black and squawking with the pestilence and beauty of them. Even the pines around the graveyard's perimeter were so thick with starlings that whole clouds of them arose and resettled when a limb grew too heavy and sank. They even sat on the curved tops of the tombstones. My father made observations about where they came from, why they chose this place to gather and grackle. Then he got that look which meant he had thought of something worth remembering.

"Watch how old C. Chaplin handles this." He handed me his drink, then worked his palms together. He eased from the car as gracefully as a cat. Before I could speak he was zigzagging into the thick of them. His cheeks quivered from the impact of his soles on the ungiving earth. "Yah!" my father yelled, hands held high and askew. "Yah-*weeee*," he hollered, his voice reaching a solid note I had never heard it reach before. I would tell Fisher that his grandfather let loose with a "yah" as fine as I ever heard as he scared those birds. Here was a man full of the noise and strength it takes to fight gravity.

I sat outside the tent remembering the look on my father's face when he had quit his running and stood amidst the eerie hushedness of things unaccountable urged upward into air. His face had the same look Fisher's had when, as a baby, I had pitched him toward the ceiling, and he got his first taste of the scary freedom of flight. Both faces had stretched into the surprised realization that here indeed was a moment against which preparation was impossible. I felt a sharp twinge at the strangers my son and I would be to each other when he grew old enough to understand all this. Then I put the bottle down and crawled inside the tent. I settled into the warm spot between their sleeping generations, and for the first time in my life I felt humbled by that ache which even pharaohs knelt down before when they saw the capstone set into place, and they yielded to how we would remember them.

My People's Waltz

I HAIL from a stock of people who dance in their kitchens. Any event which time can't accommodate—a premonition of death, the sudden realization I am loved, the hardy backslapping and hopeful hoisting of glasses at weddings, and *especially* the soft, early morning sounds certain women voice when surprised with a hungry kiss behind the ear—these moments move like ancestors through my musculature and set my feet to motion. Once, shortly after my ex-wife, Lisa, gave birth, I placed her and our son in the kitchen's most comfortable chair and swayed naked around them in Maypole fashion. "You nut," she had laughed; she still admired the prankster in me. Another time, when divorce became apparent, I made her sit in that same chair and watch me dance with my shadow. Then we uncorked some wine and rolled a fat number and held a wake over the parts of our lives that had passed. We even made love on the checkered linoleum. Afterward, I felt as if I had pirouetted through Lisa and space and landed on the far side of divorce's reality. This was my first inkling of the vanishing points love flings people through. I had actually thought our unraveling could be mended with a noisy and physical declaration of my feelings. Ours was an attachment I would later associate with the thwarted sensation of missed airplane flights and lost causes. My mother called this nagging and incurable feeling the love of last stands.

"This last stand stuff you men learn—where you make some desperate claim on someone's feelings—who teaches you that crap?" my mother asked once when I called to whine about my divorce. *"Women* don't do things like that."

But in fact, my mother held the record for the number of last stands a person could claim on someone's heart. She would pick a lingering disease and practice dying of its symptoms. I had been called home four times from as many states in the nomadic life I had lived since my divorce. The last orchestrated visit, she met me at the airport with the cheery news that she had Alzheimer's. She didn't.

"You're lucky I even remembered who you are." She had visited the hairdresser for the occasion and smelled of the beauty shop's mystery when I hugged her. "Let's have a toddy at the airport bar, I don't *think* I've had one today." During vodka tonics, she observed that none of her ex-husbands (all dead) could hold their liquor; that my son, Fisher—she produced a wallet picture—had *her* blue eyes and patrician nose; and that Dean Smith couldn't cut the mustard anymore. One of my mother's husbands had left her lifetime tickets to North Carolina basketball games, and her seats were four rows behind Coach Smith's bench.

"Dean's lost his fire." She sighed. "He never gets technicals. Not like when he was young and still screamed at some jerk referee." She sipped her drink thoughtfully through the swizzle straw and feigned remembering something by tapping her forehead with her palm. Then she informed me Lisa and Fisher would fly in the next morning; my mother had sent them tickets, and Lisa needed a little vacation to sort things. I knew through Fisher and telephone innuendos that Lisa was considering remarriage to an old high school flame who had turned up in her life again.

"Is this serious?" I had asked Lisa.

"No, it's fatal," she had said. I didn't appreciate the joke, and I had hung up.

"I should get on a plane and head back home," I said to my mother. "This is your tour de force." I raised my drink in salute.

"But you won't," my mother said. "You'll weather the weekend."

"Why didn't you at least *warn* me?"

"I've got Alzheimer's, and I'm supposed to forget things."

I remarked being in a house with a woman I once loved might be disastrous.

"Why just one woman? What about me?"

"You know what I mean."

As I drove my mother's car from the airport, she read aloud billboards. The ones on the interstate proclaimed the whole state was rocking with Carolina Fever. The portion of the state where my mother lived, along tobacco road, was thick with universities and old rivalries. When I asked if she went to the games alone or with a friend, my mother avoided the subject.

"The speed limit's seventy," she complained. "They changed it since your last visit. Speed it up." Then she began reminiscing.

"You were always the most cautious child," she said. "On Saturdays, when the fire department tested the tornado and nuclear attack horn, you made your father and me get under the kitchen table to practice what you called end-of-the-world drills. You made us cover our eyes to protect us from the flash, and then *you'd* peek. When the test pattern came on the TV or radio, you hid under the bed. After they put that FBI show on television, you wouldn't open any of the mail order knickknacks you bought, because of that episode about mail bombs. You made me open them. You always stood behind me, as if the explosion wouldn't kill us both. I never knew if you were *that* afraid of catastrophe, or if you actually believed I could shield you from it."

And I must have inherited this preoccupation with casualty from my mother. Later that afternoon, we sipped gin in the sunroom while she searched the sky with binoculars for Medivac helicopters. She claimed this wasn't a good day for her hobby; the cloud ceiling was low and brooding, and the weather reports threatened snow—rare in Haw River. I mixed martinis while my mother reminded me that my father had overseen the construction of the helicopter pads when he worked as special projects director for the county hospital. She believed he had spitefully placed the pads so that the take off and approach of the copters (her word) went over her house. She pointed to one flying treetop-low as it whumped in for landing. She claimed they flew in from the west when transporting critically ill patients to specialists in Durham or Chapel Hill and from the east when the cargo was donated organs or dead bodies.

"He wanted me to watch death fly over. He didn't know I would enjoy it." She waggled her drink at me. Any mention of my father made my mother thirsty. "Mix us another batch."

The juniper reminded me of summer and a solar eclipse I had witnessed as a child. When I awoke that morning, my father sat hunched at the kitchen table constructing a shoebox observatory. My mother kneaded his bare shoulders and hummed the last few bars of happiness left in their marriage. *It's not because I don't love you,* she had said. She toyed with his cowlick, just as Lisa would later fondle my bald spot when *we* were divorcing and adjusting to the gravity of loss. When my father saw me, he excitedly explained the physics of an eclipse. He claimed we would dance that day in the umbra of the moon. Other fathers had built observatories too, and we gathered in the street to watch celestial order pass over. Whole families congregated curbside, and drinks and fried chicken were shared, and the elderly residents remarked nothing like this would happen again in their lifetimes. Of course none of those shoeboxes worked satisfactorily, so we shielded our eyes with two pairs of sunglasses and looked upward. When someone speculated we could go blind like this, my father said that *everything* was risky business. Then the birds flew into the oaks to roost, and the corner streetlight flickered, and everyone hushed. We had stood there, my neighborhood—all of the planet I knew—caught in the shadow of the motion of heavenly bodies. *Let's dance,* my father said, and soon other couples followed. Someone pulled a car into the street and gave the radio full volume, but it seemed we were swaying to the music of the spheres. How could everyone dance when nothing—even the sun—could be trusted? I was thirteen and ignorant of endings and shifting alignments.

As I handed my mother her martini, I realized she had felt, many times, that nothing could be trusted. It saddened me to think of all the hours she had spent searching the sky for the doomed or for donated organs.

"Don't you find that depressing?" I asked.

"It beats bird watching," she said. "You don't need a manual to name what's flying over."

My mother's shopping habits were also peculiar. She rousted me at five A.M. by vacuuming the guest room where I slept. Then she explained a winter storm watch had been issued; we should hurry to the grocery store to gather provisions. When I protested, her look said she *would* have her way. The house smelled of air fresheners and scouring liquids and my son's favorite dish—clove-spiked ham. For nearly two hours, she'd been ordering her house in anticipation of what I feared would be a regretful reunion.

"We could all get snowbound here in a winter wonderland," my mother said happily as I sipped coffee in the breakfast nook. "Do you remember that time it snowed two feet, and I cooked fondue over sterno?"

"I thought people with Alzheimer's forgot things."

"It's not that advanced yet."

"It could be in remission," I suggested. Part of my mother's beauty was that she could persuade you to willingly participate in what you knew was an illusion.

We drove to an all-night supermarket whose doors opened into the empty feeling of unpeopled places. A stockboy flirting with a cashier frowned at the noise I made unsticking the cart. In the produce section, my mother spent whole minutes squeezing grapefruits for firmness and eyeing the shape of yellow onions.

"The oblong ones have more aroma." She insisted I smell the difference.

"I guess we're in this for the long haul."

"Don't be a sourpuss." She foraged through her purse and found two Valiums. "Here. Take one. They're *prescription.*"

My mother and I shared sympathies through substances. Had she offered me a slug of bourbon as we rounded aisle number three, I would have accepted, for my family survived by layering ourselves from the source of our trouble—love. My mother understood intuitively that people use each other as mirrors, and when she didn't like the image she saw, she changed partners. For this reason, she needed many men in her life. The ghost of my childhood, she was a seasonal creature given to nervous lapses and periods of hospitalization. It sobered me to think of all the hours she had spent on the psychiatrist's couch, trying to discern where happiness had ended and misfortune had tapped in. Why is it that the one thing people want to give away—loneliness—is a shared commodity and not even theirs to own? My mother seemed to sense I was pitying her, and we were both ashamed. We stood like that in the awkwardness of grocery-store muzak.

"Why don't they play something in these places you can dance to?" My mother held up items and insisted I choose the brands. "Thanks for coming home." Though her larder contained enough food for the return of three prodigals, we shopped as if we had won a spree. Anything marked family pack got tossed into the cart. We even rang the butcher bell and scolded the attendant, who explained there would be no porterhouses until the butcher came on board at eight. By the time we reached the checkout counter, the wheels of the cart groaned. My mother allowed me to win the squabble over the bill.

"Isn't that sad?" She motioned behind her. We had shopped so long and thoroughly that a group of customers had straggled in to buy milk and eggs and bread—the meager necessities everyone purchases to ward off disaster. They waited in line behind us—all of them old, with plastic handbaskets and single portions because they dined alone. Shopping with my mother had made me forget that, more nights than I cared to admit, I ate with the television as company.

THE HOUSEGUESTS arrived without their luggage, which had been rerouted to a different time zone. They fishtailed up the long driveway and scattered the starlings I was feeding while my mother stood cross-armed and supervised. The rented car had hardly stopped when my son dove into my arms.

"Our flight got changed. Our clothes are lost somewhere up there." Fisher pointed to a sky dizzy with falling snow. I danced our homecoming jig while he got his bearings by testing my face with his hands. We lived three states apart, and I had been a voice on the phone since the Christmas holidays. Didn't he need a shave too? he asked, feeding me a few lint-covered peanuts from his stash. "Look." He smiled and fingered a gap from a lost incisor.

"Did you wrestle with the wolf?"

"No, silly. The wolf didn't do this. I'm losing my baby teeth." He insisted I wiggle one so loose it flapped when he breathed hard. Then he swiveled my head by grabbing my ears. "Mom's in one of her moods," he whispered. "She told me today that all men are little boys. Does that mean all little boys are men?"

"Go give grandma a big hug." My mother hated being called that.

"Come to Nanna." My mother and Fisher went inside the house.

"Welcome, traveler," I said to Lisa in my best airport announcer's voice. "Our ground time here will be brief."

"You and your mother have been hitting the pharmaceuticals."

"None of this was my idea. And she doesn't have Alzheimer's."

"Get one thing straight," said Lisa. "I came here to think things over."

"By all means chew your cud." This was exactly the wrong thing to say. Lisa cried and informed me between sobs that Fisher was feigning stomachaches to stay home from school. When called upon in class, he pretended to be seized by a catatonic fit. How was she to cope with this alone, Lisa wanted to know? *I* didn't have to face the daily catastrophes of parenting. I got to be Mister Good Guy—camping trips and phone calls and vacations. She had to juggle all this with a teaching job and with starting a new life while she was afraid of making old mistakes. She thought my confusion was a smirk. "You're glad I feel like this."

"I don't wish misfortune on anyone."

"No, but you sure take an I-told-you-so attitude when it happens." She looked up at the swirling snow. "Shit. All this and lost clothes. My mascara's running, and I want a cigarette."

"I thought you and what's-his-name went on the patch."

"Royce," she said. "His name is Royce, and yes, we quit smoking, but right now I want a cigarette. Please, Richard. Smoke one *for* me."

I did. I lit up a Camel and inhaled to my toes for my ex-wife. Talk was not necessary; we were remembering. How do our hopeful histories ever get so sadly jumbled? I recollected a fishing trip along the White River in Arkansas. Though divorced, we still shared vacations and the pretense of being a family. I had purposefully stumbled into the campsite's unisex bath facility where Lisa was singing as she showered. For a quick instant, she had looked at me in terror—as if I were a man armed with harm. *It's just me,* I had said. She stood in clouds of steam, shielding her breasts and pubis. *You can't see me like this anymore,* she had said. This was how I felt now, like a trespasser. I extinguished the half-smoked cigarette.

"Are you seeing anyone?" Lisa asked. "You should be."

"I'm over you," I said to Lisa. "I'm hooked up with a whole series of vixens."

"You were never a good liar. Royce has asked me to marry him."

"What does Fisher say about all this?"

"Fisher understands. When will you?"

My mother would receive her winter wonderland. By afternoon, the local announcer was calling the snowstorm a blizzard and offering tips against hypothermia. Six meager inches had fallen. Between cocktails and rewindings of *Star Wars,* my mother rummaged through closets for navy blankets and quilts and pillows lumpy with discarded use. From somewhere, she found a ten-pound bag of salt and a snow shovel. She made me fill containers with water in case the pipes froze. Soon, the living room resembled a garage sale. She even produced a box of dusty flares.

"Cool." Fisher emerged from a tent built over furniture. "We can light these later if we have an emergency."

"We'll have to sleep in here tonight, like early pioneers, if the power goes." Then my mother worried aloud that she had forgotten where she stored the air mattresses.

"This is sort of romantic." Lisa's second martini had settled in, and she had called Royce, who had *insisted* (her word) she fly here and deliver the good news face to face so that *closure* could be formulated. Evidently, this guy Royce had none of my outlandish characteristics. Lisa admired the fire I had built. "Not romantic in the sense of courtship, but in the sense of an adventure."

"If the TV quits, I've got a Ouija board," my mother said happily. "We could talk to spirits." She toyed with an amulet I had never seen.

"What's that thing?" Had she placed her faith in crystals and past lives?

She said it was her Lifeline, though she was embarrassed to wear it in public as it made her feel old and frail. She explained the little device gave off a beep and an electronic signal which alerted rescuers to the emergency. She told the story of a neighbor named Hazel who had sixteen cats. Hazel had outlived all her relatives, and she had a reputation for poisoning neighborhood dogs which wandered onto her property. On Christmas, Hazel threw firecrackers at carolers. Who hasn't heard a version of this story? In another rendition, pigs in a pen might replace the cats, or an old hunchback might stand in for the witch, but in the end the miser dies utterly alone, and the corpse becomes a macabre feast. The fear of death's loneliness is central to each telling. In my mother's account, the cats ate the face off poor Hazel before a collecting paperboy found her.

"That's why I have this Lifeline," my mother said.

"You don't own any cats," I pointed out.

"That's beside the point."

"Mice," Fisher said. "Mice could eat your face off."

"That's exactly right," said my mother. "Mice could make your face look like Swiss cheese, and I *will not* meet my Maker like that. But then, Fisher, your father doesn't believe in a Maker. He went to college and became an atheist."

"All I said was that you don't have any cats."

"Dad, do Atheists believe in the Pledge of Allegiance? At school, this one guy has a note from his parents, and he doesn't have to recite it."

"This thing connects me with security," my mother said.

"I wasn't bashing Lifeline."

"How *do* you think we're all connected?" asked Lisa.

Her question unmoored me. "Honey," I said. "It's just that, and I'm sorry to admit this, I don't know how to shape the words for what I feel sometimes."

So I tried to frame my answer inside a story. I explained being en route with Fisher on vacation. He and I usually stopped at a campground beside a flat stretch of the interstate, where on hot days mirages were created. Big trucks and vans with whole families seemed to arise from nowhere and swoosh past and disappear. The campground had a stocked pond and a little dock from which we watched and fished and practiced the art of knot tying. I taught Fisher clinch, surgeon's and blood knots. Each knot came with a story about some family member now dead. In the retelling of some cockeyed adventure like arrowhead hunting or all-you-could-eat ribs after fasting for an entire day, I'd watch Fisher and feel like a memory to myself. That day, there seemed no greater power than the confluence his fingers would remember whenever they tied knots.

"Knots," I said finally. "Knots are how we are connected."

"He's looped," my mother said. "He could never handle prescriptions."

"I know," Lisa said. The gentleness in both their voices amazed me. Why is it that, when you explain a part of the story of yourself, it's like trying to clinch the loose ends of air?

AT DUSK, I decided to walk around my old neighborhood. Fisher began crying because his snow clothes were lost in the sky. My mother explained she had to have something a little man could wear. When they returned from the attic, he was dressed like a child playing grown-up. Wool socks fit over his hands instead of mittens, and a flowery housecoat cut in half was pinned to make a hasty jumpsuit. Plastic bags were duct-taped over his tennis shoes, and a fur muffler served as a hat. He screeched on the flute he had found.

"I'm the pied piper," he said once we were outside. "Look. Now it's a smoking pipe." His breath steamed from the finger holes.

We walked down streets where I had once been a paperboy. Ours had been a subdivision in which people had invested, then fled. The land, once rural, was now suburban. Most of the three-bedroom houses were brick veneer and grouped in clusters on property old man Teague sold as his senile whimsy saw fit. He shared his house with chickens which roosted in the kitchen, and his yard was rumored to contain a fortune buried in coffee cans. Apartment complexes now squatted where his house and the woods of my childhood once stood. Old man Teague scared me so much that, as his paperboy, I rarely collected. When I told this story to Fisher, he laughed at my foolishness. He claimed he would have snuck in at night and dug up the buried treasure.

"But first, I would have found the map the old guy drew. The one they always draw with X marking the spot." A man driving by in a minivan with chains slowed and flung out his arm, so my son and I waved. I anticipated a brief encounter in which he would recognize me as someone who was reared here. We would swap anecdotes. It didn't happen. He ignored us and tossed a bagged newspaper in a driveway. The difference between the missing worlds of paperboys and papermen struck me.

"Look at that." We had circled the block, and Fisher pointed to a neighbor's clothesline. He had never seen frozen clothes before—he lived too far south—and he lumbered through the snow to test their cardboard feel. He remarked that they felt different at this temperature than when freshly laundered and worn. He batted a neighbor's boxers like a piñata.

"Weird." This was his term for anything interesting. When I explained they would thaw out, he seemed disappointed. "We could steal them. *Our* clothes got stolen."

That word—"steal"—shook me. What divorced father hasn't considered stealing his child? I had even charted an escape route and ordered brochures from friendly sounding cities. We would live by guile and rove through America under assumed names like righteous outlaws. The imagined image of his face on a milk carton had kept me from felony. How could I kidnap this part of myself which was mine to name, but not to own? I explained to Fisher that the airport would return their clothes, that stealing was wrong, but that we could leave a little surprise for the owners.

He fashioned the wet snow easily into a ball which we rolled. Fisher giggled excitedly as we made a snowman. In the innocence of that sound, I heard his mother's laughter. Once, she and I had found a wallet on the White River while camping. Fisher was just an urge between us then, which our union would cre-

ate. I couldn't even remember if we were married or living together or engaged—but we were happy, and we were in love—
I did know that. Inside the wallet were a driver's license, credit
cards, pictures of loved ones, and a bobby pin which had mean-
ing enough for its owner to save. There was also a hundred bucks
inside. Here was good fortune, and it was ours. When Lisa wondered if the man had drowned, I had observed that, if so, he
didn't need the money. Those twenties got us a cozy motel room,
a restaurant meal with steaks and champagne, and the feeling
that we would always be beneficiaries. *We're like Bonnie and Clyde,*
Lisa had giggled as I overtipped the waiter. The wallet belonged
to Clyde Lockhart, and we laughed over that, full of the thievery of love. We had mailed the billfold back in an envelope with
no return address and a photo-booth picture of us kissing. I wondered what that stranger named Clyde Lockhart thought when
he opened the envelope. Did he curse the missing one hundred
or give thanks because something had been returned? Did our
picture remind him of his reasons for keeping that bobby pin?

"Help me make this snowman," Fisher said.

"Snowperson." I slapped on two breasts. He added three more,
and we gave it many stick arms and extra faces like Siva. Then we
clothed it beggar fashion. We used boxers as a hat, socks as a
fringe on a hula skirt, and a negligee as a cape for flying.

"I bet the neighbors think spirits did this," Fisher said. He
even talked to the urge of his creation, and in his voice I heard
inklings of the first time he would wake beside someone newly
beloved. A streetlight near where we worked had flickered on,
and he looked up into the hush from which snow falls.

"Weird," he said, and we both understood the new ways old
feelings get laundered.

THE ONLY spirits we would contact that night were the gods
which move people to dance in kitchens. Upon returning, Fisher

and I found Lisa and my mother at the Ouija board, quite drunk and debating on the protocol for getting it to work. Did you ask the questions aloud or silently, like a prayer? Should all of us place our fingers on the planchette, or was this a game for only two? My mother had lost the directions, and no one could recollect. The feast she had prepared sat around them, unattended. Here were palm-sized slabs of marbled ham, assorted pickles and olives, deviled eggs and aged cheeses, and two braided loaves of bread which smelled of yeast and promise. Here was God's plenty, and no one touched it.

"Sit down and help," Lisa said. "We can't even remember if ghosts talk in sentences or cryptoquotes."

"Don't mind us, we're smashed." My mother twirled the Lifeline amulet like a coach's whistle. "You know, I can't recall this game ever giving up any real answers."

"You have to ask it easy stuff," Fisher said. "Ask will we be happy. Then we'll make it say yes."

"I don't even remember who gave me this, or the occasion," my mother said. "Do you think I got it on Valentine's Day, or Halloween?"

Then Fisher reminded us it was not day anymore, but night and time for supper. How had we forgotten something as simple as human appetite, I wondered? When he and I washed up, he confided the Ouija board scared him.

"What are you afraid of?" I asked.

"Of knowing things I don't want to know." Once, after a particularly bad argument with Lisa in Texas, I had taken Fisher on a walk. Though a small man, I step quickly when angered, and I hear only the murderous voices in my head. Five minutes into my choler, I heard Fisher trying to hide his crying. I thought he was cold and took him into my arms. "I'm afraid, Dad," he had said. We were walking past a pasture, where unseen cows made noises as they hunkered against the weather. He had thought they were the voices of hoodoo, calling. How do you explain to your son we all battle the same monsters under our beds?

"Grownups are afraid of the same thing," I said to Fisher. "I'm not sure if you ever get used to it."

Back in the kitchen, we cast aside the game board which promised answers. We sat down at that table and laid waste as if the supper were our last. My mother un-newspapered the good china from her marriages, and no one complained that the designs were mismatched or that a few edges were chipped. We filled crystal pitchers with buttermilk, leaded glasses with liqueurs, and whole bottles of wine got unstoppered and aired.

"Let's do this stuff backwards," Fisher said, and we did. We ate dessert first, we made ham sandwiches with mustard on the outside, and we even sat at the table with the chairs facing outward. We used spoons as forks and napkins as crazy helmets. We called it topsy-turvy time, and it was as if some solstice had shifted us on our axis.

"Look!" Fisher had crunched into a Captain's Wafer and lost his wiggly tooth. He held it up as if he had found lost gold, while his tongue tested the new feel of a space where something more permanent would grow. Lisa remembered aloud he must be exhausted from the trip, and she seized upon the old promise of the tooth fairy to shepherd him to bed. I followed her to stoke the living room fire and help with the tucking-in. They took foil and ribbon and a little piece of paper with them.

"Don't you just put it under the pillow?" I asked.

"No, Dad. You have to wrap it up like a present and leave a little note with a good wish on it." There was no hint of suspicion in his voice.

"I guess I forgot," I said.

"That's okay." He yawned once and fell asleep.

"I don't know how things like this work," I said to Lisa.

"You make them up as you go along, silly."

I stood back and admired this woman I had married. When she kissed our son on his forehead, she hooked her hair behind her ears in a manner I had grown to love. The slope of her blouse gave way gracefully to her neck and highlighted her clavicle. Underneath were breasts whose firm gravity my hand had admired and three moles the color of rich earth.

"Let me ask you something," I said. "If you knew when we married what we know now—that we would divorce—if you knew that, would you still do it all over again?"

"Richard," she said. "I loved you. Sometimes that just isn't enough."

I wish these were the stories of people who cavorted more with happiness than with the moments from which they needed rescue. I wish my people were more nimble and sure-footed. I wish we did not orbit around the confused music of our hearts. All my people have ever aspired toward was a place where the geography of ourselves made sense.

But what I can explain is how we danced that night. Lisa and I were watching Fisher sleep when my mother's Lifeline began beeping like a pager gone berserk. We rushed into the kitchen and found my mother on her back, convulsing. I was about to pound on her chest when she sat up, laughing.

"Gotcha," she said. This was the only practical joke she had ever pulled.

When the phone rang, I answered it. "Lifeline!" a lady yelled. "Do I need to send the rescue unit? Is someone having a fit, or are they dying?"

"No, ma'am," I said. "We just wanted to see if this thing worked. My mother set it off accidentally."

"It's *Lifeline*," the lady screamed. "It's not a toy."

I found my drink and washed down her exasperation. "We didn't mean to play with something so serious." Then I explained my mother had Alzheimer's and had forgotten what the thing was. My mother and Lisa were in hysterics.

"You all sound drunk and dysfunctional." She hung up noisily.

Who knows what restores us to our upper regions—that place in our natures where love and other old quarrels seem like little trespasses when compared to our ancient dispute with the earth we are made of and our short stomp upon it. For me, it was a simple power outage. The lights flickered, and then the house went dark as the electricity died.

"The power went." My mother was happy to be right. Our commotion had woken Fisher, who came into the kitchen with the flashlights and radio he had stockpiled. Lisa found an easy-listening station while my mother lit candles.

"It's been so long since I danced in my own house," said my mother. She claimed she wanted to feel like a kid, running through a sprinkler.

What can you do sometimes but sway to the grave sensation of the world moving through you? I understood why my father made those clumsy shoebox observatories—to hold motion in his hands. My mother would die of a stroke within a year, not of imagined Alzheimer's. Two mornings later, Lisa and I would take separate flights to our distant lives. I swear, though we were some five miles from the Haw River that night, I could hear the force of its flowing hymn. It sounded like the noisy hush of a congregation, rising to greet where Sunday or circumstance had driven them. Just as a storyteller gives voice to a lost part of himself when he tells a tale, this night would get absorbed into the dance steps Fisher would half-remember some shadowy summer evening for *his* children. What would he reinvent of me and all the bare instants through which we fluctuate? Such waltzing would not always be easy; it would require hard choices, and more than once he would duet with disaster. My heart ached for yet envied all the complicated footwork he would master to keep the wolf from his door.

"Come on, Dad," he said. *"Dance."*

I stepped forth into a generous space, where brief gestures mattered. I did my best cakewalk toward my loved ones in that room where our voices echoed, and then were gone.

Made in the USA
Lexington, KY
26 July 2014